"This is happening too fast, Mick. Can't you see that? Can't you see that I've never—"

Lorna paused, turned away again.

"Never what? Felt like this before?" Mick said, right on her heels. "'Cause that's the way I'm feeling. Like I've been hit by lightning."

"Or lived through a storm," she said, almost to herself. That's exactly what it felt like, being with him, being in his arms—as if she was reliving the storm all over again....

Books by Lenora Worth

Love Inspired

The Wedding Quilt #12
Logan's Child #26
I'll Be Home for Christmas #44
Wedding at Wildwood #53
His Brother's Wife #82
Ben's Bundle of Joy #99
The Reluctant Hero #108
One Golden Christmas #122
When Love Came to Town #142

LENORA WORTH

grew up in a small Georgia town and decided in the fourth grade that she wanted to be a writer. But first she married her high school sweetheart, then moved to Atlanta, Georgia. Taking care of their baby daughter at home while her husband worked at night, Lenora discovered the world of romance novels and knew that's what she wanted to write. And so she began.

A few years later, the family settled in Shreveport, Louisiana, where Lenora continued to write while working as a marketing assistant. After the birth of her second child, a boy, she decided to pursue her dream full-time. In 1993 Lenora's hard work and determination finally paid off with that first sale.

"I never gave up, and I believe my faith in God helped get me through the rough times when I doubted myself," Lenora says. "Each time I start a new book, I say a prayer, asking God to give me the strength and direction to put the words to paper. That's why I'm so thrilled to be a part of Steeple Hill's Love Inspired line, where I can combine my faith in God with my love of romance. It's the best combination."

When Love
Came to Town
Lenora Worth

Love Inspired®

Published by Steeple Hill Books™

STEEPLE HILL BOOKS

Steeple
Hill™

ISBN 0-373-87149-X

WHEN LOVE CAME TO TOWN

You shall hide them in the secret place of Your presence, from the plots of man; You shall keep them secretly in a pavilion....

—*Psalms* 31:20

To my niece Rhonda, with love
And...to all the Hildas of the world

Chapter One

"**B**oys, we've got ourselves one big mess here."

Mick Love looked around at the devastation and destruction, wondering how anyone had survived the predawn tornado that had hit the small town of Jardin, Louisiana, more than twenty-four hours ago. He understood why his friend at the power company had called him and his crew to come to the rescue.

Due to a nasty storm churning in the Gulf of Mexico, a series of powerful thunderstorms had rolled through most of Louisiana, leaving enough damage to tie up the local power companies for days to come. Both the governor and the president had declared the state a disaster area, so utilities workers from Texas and Mississippi had been called in to help.

Apparently, Jardin had been one of the worst-hit spots this side of the Mississippi River. Trees were down all across the tight-knit rural community, causing power outages and damage to many homes and businesses. This particular spot had suffered some of the worst damage Mick had seen. Just two days ago, the vast acreage had been breathtakingly beautiful, an historical showplace that attracted hundreds of tourists during the spring and summer when its gardens were in full bloom.

But not today. Today, the fertile, riotous gardens looked as if they'd been trampled and smashed by a giant's foot, the tender pink- and salmon-colored azalea blooms and crushed bloodred rose petals dropped across the green grass like torn bits of old lace. Heavy magnolia branches and limbs from the live oaks, some of them hundreds of years old, lay bent and twisted, exposed, across the lush, flat lawn. And everywhere, broken blossoms and hurled bushes lay crushed and bruised amid the split, shattered oaks of Bayou le Jardin.

Bayou le Jardin. The Garden in the Bayou, as some of the locals liked to call this place. Mick glanced back up at the house that stood towering over him like something out of a period movie set. Right now, the white-columned, pink-walled stucco mansion with its wraparound galleries and green-shuttered French doors looked as if Sherman himself had marched right through it. Shutters and roof tiles dangled amid the rubble of tree limbs and broken flower blossoms. A fat brown-black tree limb had just clipped one of the dormer windows on the third floor, taking part of the roof with it.

And yet, the house had somehow survived the wrath of the storm. Mick had to wonder just what else this centuries-old house had survived.

No time for daydreaming about that now though. He had work to do. Lots of work.

"Okay, let's get this show on the road," he called, issuing orders as he pulled his yellow hard hat low on his brow, his heavy leather work gloves clutched in one hand. "This won't be easy, but we've got to get these trees off those lines and out of this yard and driveway."

Soon, his crew was hard at work, cutting and removing some of the smaller limbs. These great oaks shot up to well over forty-feet high, and some of the limbs measured wider than a man's waist. Luckily, though, only a few of the thirty or so huge oaks had suffered damage. And most of those were in the back gardens.

Deciding things were well under control here, Mick headed around the front of the huge house. He wanted to see what needed to be done with the few broken limbs along the great alley of oaks that lined the driveway up to the house from the Old River Road that followed the Mississippi River.

In the back gardens, people were buzzing around here and there. Utility workers, concerned tourists and employees of the popular bed-and-breakfast—all hurried and hustled, some of them underfoot, some of them offering to help out where they could.

But now, as Mick came around the corner and into the long, wide front yard, he looked up to see one lone figure standing a few feet away, underneath the canopy of the double row of towering oaks.

Right underneath a broken limb that was hanging by mere splinters from a massive tree.

Mick squinted, then waved a hand as he ran toward the person—who looked like a teenager, decked out in jeans and a big T-shirt, an oversized baseball cap covering his head. That cap wouldn't help if the limb fell on him.

Which is why Mick waved and shouted. "Hey, little fellow, be careful out there. Watch for those limbs—"

The wind picked up. The hanging limb moved precariously, then with a shudder began to let go of the branch to which it had clung.

Mick didn't even think. He just dived for the tiny figure in front of him, knocking the boy and himself to the wet ground as the limb crashed to the very spot where the teenager had been standing.

Winded and angry, Mick turned from the still-shaking leafy limb, tickling and teasing just inches from his feet, to the body crushed underneath his, fully prepared to tell this interloper to save himself and everyone else some grief by getting out of the way.

And looked down to find another surprise.

This was no boy. No teenager, either. The cap had fallen off in the scuffle, only to reveal layers of long, thick red-blond hair. And incredible eyes.

Green. A pure and clean green like freshly mowed grass—and they looked every bit as angry as Mick felt. Maybe even more angry.

"I'm not a 'little fellow,'" she said in a voice that moved between southern sultry and cultured classy. "And I'd really appreciate it if you'd get off me. Now."

Mick rolled away as if he'd been burned by a dancing electrical wire. "Sorry, ma'am," he said, his Mississippi drawl making the words sound too slow to his own ears.

Then he glanced over at her, watching as she sat up and lifted that veil of hair off her shoulders. It rippled and fell in soft strawberry blond-colored waves and curls down her back.

Regaining some of his anger, he said, "Well, you should have enough sense not to stand underneath a broken limb like that, little fellow or not."

Blowing red-gold bangs out of her mad green eyes, the woman got up and brushed off her bottom, then grabbed her bright purple-and-yellow LSU baseball cap, her eyes flashing like a lightning bolt. With a long sigh, she tried with little success to pull all that hair up into a haphazard ball so she could put her hat back on. Finally giving up, she let her hair drop back down her back, then plopped the hat against her leg in frustration. "I was surveying my property. And just who are you, anyway?"

Her property. Mick gave her the once-over again, then grinned. "Don't tell me you're Aunt Hilda? Hilda Dorsette?"

"Hardly," she replied in a haughty tone, still flapping her hat against her damp jeans. An expression bordering on arrogant moved across her delicately freckled face. "I'm Lorna Dorsette, her niece. And I believe I asked you first."

"So you did," he said, still grinning, his heart still beating hard after that near collision with the limb. Or maybe because of the beautiful, petite woman standing in front of him. Extending his muddy hand, he said, "Mick Love."

She ignored his hand, then glanced at his hard hat, which had landed on the ground a few feet away, her neck craned as she read the bold black lettering stamped across the front. "Love's Tree Service?"

"That's me. Claude Juneau called us yesterday. Said you had some major tree problems out here."

She relaxed a bit, then nodded. "Claude and his crew took care of the worst of the power lines, so we do have electricity now, at least. But they had too much to handle to bother with the tree limbs. He said he'd have to call in reinforcements from Mississippi."

"That'd be me," Mick said, extending his hand

again in what he hoped would be forgiveness. "I'm sorry I knocked you down, Miz Dorsette."

"It's Lorna," she said, returning his handshake with a firm, no-nonsense grip. "And I appreciate your concern." Glancing over at the jumbled mass of branches and leaves behind him, she added, "I didn't realize the limb was so badly broken."

"Could have been worse," Mick replied, as they turned to head back toward the mansion. "The backyard sure is bad off. It's gonna take us a few days to get it cleared up."

Lorna nodded again. "When I heard your trucks pulling up, I threw on some clothes and came out to supervise." She stopped walking, then looked up at the house. "But the sight just made me so sick to my stomach. I had to find a quiet spot."

To compose herself, Mick reasoned. Lorna Dorsette didn't strike him as the type to burst into tears, but he reckoned from the flash of anger he'd seen in her eyes earlier, she'd gladly throw a fit or two. Yeah, she'd probably just grit her teeth and keep on going, telling everyone exactly what she thought. Even through a disaster such as this. What, besides being a glorious redhead, had made her so strong-minded? he wondered.

"I understand," he said. "These spring storms can really do some damage, and this one was a doozy. It's hard to look at, when it's your own place."

She turned back to him then, her face composed

and calm, shimmering from the building early morning humidity. "Yes, but we're blessed that no one got hurt or killed—some did in other parts of the state. We've mostly got property damage. That, at least, can be repaired."

Mick didn't miss the darkness in her eyes. Or the way she'd almost whispered that last statement. Curious, and against his better judgment, he asked, "What exactly were you doing out there underneath those big old trees?"

Lorna put both hands on her hips, then gave him a direct look. "Praying, Mr. Love. Just praying."

That floored him. The intense honesty in her eyes left no room for doubt. And made Mick feel foolish. Most of the women he knew rarely prayed. This woman was as serious as the big trees shading them from the sun. And apparently, just as rooted. A provincial country girl. Quaint and pretty. And toting religion. Double trouble.

Which only made Mick, the wanderer, the unsettled bachelor, doubly intrigued.

When he didn't speak, she lifted her head a notch. "Do you pray, Mr. Love?"

"Call me Mick," he said, all of a sudden too hot and uncomfortable to be reasonable. "Does it matter if I do or don't? I'll still get the job done."

Her smile made him edgy and immediately put him on alert. "Yes, it matters. Aunt Hilda will have you out in the garden in a heartbeat, reciting the 'Lord's Prayer' if she finds out you don't pray."

"Oh, I see." He laughed, relieved to see that she had a sense of humor right along with her sense of piety. "So you pray to impress your aunt?"

"No, I pray to remain close to God," Lorna explained, slowly and in that voice that poured like soft rain over Mick's nerve endings. "We have a tradition here at Bayou le Jardin. We take our troubles to the garden. And there we walk and talk with God. It's based on my aunt's favorite hymn."

Okay, so he'd just stumbled on a praying, hymn-singing, petite redhead with eyes that looked like green pastures. But Mick couldn't help being cynical. "Well, that's nice, but what did God tell you to do about these broken limbs and destroyed property?"

She smiled at him then, and brought his heart hammering to his feet. "He told me He'd send you."

Floored, dazed, winded, Mick couldn't think of a snappy reply. Until he remembered he'd saved her butt from that limb. That gave him some much-needed confidence.

Glancing up at the gaping open space where the limb had once hung, he said, "And just in the nick of time, I do believe."

Lorna only smiled and stared. "That remains to be seen, but yes, I guess you did come to my rescue back there."

"And don't you forget it," he retorted, glad to be

back on a human level of understanding. All this business about walking and talking with God made him jumpy.

"Oh, I won't." She marched ahead of him around the corner, her faded navy tennis shoes and frayed jeans making a nice melody of sounds as she walked.

The nice melody ended on the next beat, however, when she groaned and whirled to glare up at Mick. "Just what in blazes are your men doing to my beautiful gardens, Mr. Love?"

"Lorna's out there pitching a fit," her older sister Lacey said as she watched from the open dining room doors. "Think I should go play referee?"

Hilda Dorsette reached for her silver-etched walking cane, then slowly made her way to the French doors leading out onto the flat stone gallery. Without a word, she watched as her great-niece went nose to nose with the handsome man named Mick Love. Then she chuckled. "Good thing he's wearing that hard hat. He'll need protection from Lorna. She sets such high store in those live oaks."

Lacey shrugged, her floral sundress rippling as she moved away from the window. "He'll need more than a hard hat if he damages those gardens. I'll be right there with Lorna, fighting him."

Hilda gave Lacey a fierce stare. "The man came here to do a job, dear. The gardens are already damaged beyond repair from the storm. What more can he possibly do? He's trying to clear things up.''

Lacey heard her sister's raised voice coming through loud and clear from the many open doors and windows. ''But you know Lorna thinks she has to be the one in charge. She's obviously upset because his crew with all that big equipment has just about mashed what little garden we have left.''

''The garden will grow again,'' Hilda replied. ''It always does.''

Lacey turned back from checking the urn of strong coffee Hilda had suggested they brew for the workers and few remaining guests. ''Lorna needs to get in here and see to breakfast. They'll all be hungry.''

''Rosie Lee has breakfast well under control,'' Hilda reminded her over her shoulder. Even as she said the words, they could hear dishes rattling in the large industrial-sized kitchen located off the main dining room. ''Lacey, calm down. We're all going to make it through this.''

''I'm calm,'' Lacey retorted, then rubbed her forehead to ward off the headache clamoring for attention. ''I'm calm, Aunt Hilda.''

But she knew in her heart that she wasn't calm. How could any of them be calm after surviving the intensity of that storm? No wonder Lorna was taking out her anger on the very man who'd come to help them. It was Lorna's way of dealing with the situation, of finding some sort of control over the chaos.

Because they both knew only too well that, in the end, they had no control over either joy or tragedy.

When her baby sister's heated words turned from English to French, however, Lacey knew it was time to take the matter into her own hands. "I'm going out there," she told Hilda as she brushed past her. "I'll drag her in here by her hair if I have to."

Hilda stood leaning on her cane, her chuckle echoing after Lacey. "Maybe our Lorna has finally met her match."

Lacey didn't find that so amusing, but it would serve Lorna right if this Mick Love brought her down a peg or two. Lorna loved to boss people around, and she loved being the center of attention. Lacey was used to reining in her firebrand little sister, and, truth be told, she was getting mighty tired of it. How their brother Lucas could just take off and paddle away in his pirogue, heading out into the swamps and leaving Lacey to cover things, was beyond her. But then, she was the oldest and used to handling things.

"Lorna, we can hear you all the way to the river," she said now as she made her way through branches and bramble.

Lorna turned to find her big sister standing with her hands on her hips, that disapproving look on her lovely face. Lacey, looking so cool and collected in her sundress and upswept hair, only added to Lorna's aggravation. "Well, I don't care who can hear me.

This man and his big machines! Look what they're doing to the garden, Lacey. *Je voudrais*—''

Mick held up a hand. "Don't start that French again. If I'm being told off, I'd like it in plain English, please."

Lorna ground her teeth and dug her sneakers in for a good fight. Deep down, she knew she was making a scene. Deep down, she realized she was still in shock from the storm and the tremendous damage it had left in its wake. Deep down, in the spot where she'd buried her most horrific memories, in a place she refused to visit, in the dark place she denied with each waking breath, her emotions boiled and threatened to spill forth like a volcano about to erupt. And the storm and Mick Love had both provoked that hidden spot, bringing some of her angst right to the surface. It didn't help that she'd purposely gone out underneath the trees to find some semblance of peace, only to be broadsided by both a limb and a handsome stranger. It didn't help that she hadn't even had her coffee yet.

She let out a long-suffering sigh, then returned to English. "I would like…" She stopped, took time to relax, find control. "I would like for the past day or so to go away. I want my trees back, I want my garden intact again."

She couldn't stand the sympathy she saw in Mick Love's deep blue eyes. So she ignored it. And the way the memory of his hands on her, his body falling across hers to protect her, kept coming back to bother her when she only wanted to take out her anger on someone. Anyone. Him.

"I can't fix your garden until we get these trees out of here," Mick told her, his hands held out palm down, his head bent as if he were trying to deal with a child.

"I understand that," Lorna said, trying to be reasonable. "But do you have to stomp and shove everything that is still intact. Look at that big truck over there. They pulled it right up on top of that camellia bush. That bush has been there for over a hundred years, Mr. Love."

"And if you let me do my job, I guarantee it will be there for a hundred more years, at least," he told her, all traces of sympathy gone now. "How can you expect us to clean this up, if we don't get right in there on top of those trees and limbs?"

"It's a reasonable request, Lorna," Lacey said from behind her, a firm grip on her shoulder. "Come inside and get something to eat."

"I'm not hungry," Lorna huffed back. Her sister, always the mother hen. "But I could use a cup of coffee."

"Then let's find you one. And you, too, Mr. Love," Lacey said, her voice so cultured and cool that Lorna wanted to throw up. Whereas Lorna pretended to be calm and in control, her sister's serene countenance was no act. Lacey had it down pat. She never wavered. She never threw fits.

Lorna tossed her scorn back in Mick Love's face, daring him to make nice. She had only just begun to make a scene.

He didn't seem willing to take that dare. Eyeing Lorna with those arresting blue eyes, he said, "I don't think—"

"I insist," Lacey said, shooting Lorna a warning glare. "Come onto the gallery so we can talk. I want you to meet our aunt Hilda, anyway. You can explain to all of us exactly how you plan on clearing away all this debris."

"Would that calm *her* down?" he asked, glaring at Lorna.

Lorna didn't flinch, but that heated blue-velvet gaze did make a delicate shudder move down her spine.

"I think the coffee would help immensely," Lacey stated, pinching Lorna to make her behave. "And some kind of explanation would certainly put all of us at ease. This has been so traumatic—we thought surely we were going to be blown into the swamp. I think we're all still in shock."

"Obviously," Mick replied, his gaze shifting from Lorna to Lacey.

Lorna watched as Mick listened to her sister. Oh, he'd probably fall for Lacey's charms, bait and hook. Lacey did have a way of nurturing even the most savage of beasts. And Lorna had a way of sending men running. No, she didn't send them running, she just sent them away. Period.

Oh, she didn't need this right now. The bed-and-breakfast mansion was booked solid for the spring season, and the Garden Restaurant located out back was always busy. But what choice did she have? They had to get things cleared up.

Feeling contrite, Lorna turned back to Mick. "I'm sorry. I'm at a loss as to what to do next, and I took it out on you. We do appreciate your help."

Mick's expression seemed to relax then. He had a little-boy face, tanned and energetic, playful and challenging. Mischievous, as Aunt Hilda would say.

And tempting. Very tempting. Like a rich pastry, or a fine piece of ripe forbidden fruit.

"Apology accepted," he said. "And coffee would be most welcome."

"Then come on inside," Lacey told him, giving Lorna a nudge toward the gallery.

"Let me just talk to my men a minute," Mick replied. "I'll be right back."

Lorna watched as Mick instructed one of the men, his hard hat in his hand. He had thick, curly ash-brown hair, sunny in spots and as rich as tree bark in others.

"Don't break a stitch staring at him," Lacey warned.

"Don't pop a button telling me what to do," Lorna retorted.

Then she gasped in surprise. The man Mick had been talking to headed to one of the big white equipment-laden trucks they'd pulled into the backyard— the truck parked over the camellia bush.

"He's moving the truck," Lacey whispered. "Lorna, do you see?"

"I have eyes," Lorna stated, her hands on her hips, her brow lifted. Her heart picking up its tempo.

She looked from the groaning, grinding truck to Mick Love's gentle, gracious eyes. And felt as if the storm was still raging around her.

She had eyes, all right. But she could see right through Mick Love's kind gesture. Kindness always came with a price, didn't it?

And Lorna had to wonder just what Mick Love expected in return for *this* kindness.

Chapter Two

He had expected the strong coffee. Louisiana was famous for that. And he had expected the house to be big, cool and gracious. It had once been a plantation house and now served as an historical bed-and-breakfast vacation spot. But what Mick hadn't expected was the fierce intelligence and remarkable strength of the three women sitting out on the gallery having breakfast with him.

Nor had he expected to be extremely smitten by the very one who'd chewed him out in two different languages not an hour ago.

But then, Mick was beginning to expect the unexpected at Bayou le Jardin.

"Have your men had enough to eat, Mr. Love?"

He glanced over at Hilda Dorsette. The breakfast of French toast, biscuits, ham, grits and eggs, and fresh fruit had been more than enough. "Yes, ma'am, I think they've eaten their fill. And we sure appreciate your giving us breakfast. We cranked up in the middle of the night to get here by daylight."

"Well, we appreciate your willingness to help out," the older woman replied as she watched several of the workers going about their jobs.

Mick gave a slight nod while keeping a watchful eye on the bucket trucks. As he watched the rookie named David spike a tree so he could climb it, he added, "Claude Juneau and I go way back. I didn't mind helping him out one bit. Just sorry for the noise and clutter."

"What noise? What clutter?" The teasing light in her eyes made Mick relax, even as another chain saw cranked up and went to work on cutting up a big limb.

Mick figured the noisy wenches, stomp cutters and wood chippers would frazzle anybody's nerves. But Hilda Dorsette sat sipping her coffee as if she had heavy equipment in her fragile garden every day of the week.

Mick liked Aunt Hilda. She was plumb, petite and no-nonsense. And she was the mayor of the nearby town of Jardin—another unexpected revelation. Dressed in a bright salmon-colored casual top and a sturdy khaki flared skirt, she looked ready to take on the day. With her coiffured silver-gray hair and bright blue eyes, she was a charmer. And shrewd, too.

"I'm glad you took the time to explain the work

you're doing," she told him. "I've heard of tree services and tree surgeons, of course. We've had a local tree expert watching over our great oaks for years now. But I never knew utility companies rely on companies such as yours to help them out of tight spots."

With that statement, she finished the last of her coffee, then set the delicate china cup down on its matching saucer. "Since we seem to be in your capable hands, I'm going to leave the girls in charge while I let Tobbie drive me into the village to see what else needs to be done there. I'm sure the Mayor's Office will be hopping with activity again this morning, and my assistant Kathryn is already there waiting on me. We have to coordinate the Red Cross efforts and make sure everyone is fed and sheltered. So many people lost everything." She shook her head, then rose from the white wrought-iron chair. "I am so very thankful that Bayou le Jardin only lost trees and some of the storage buildings. It could have been much, much worse."

Mick got up as she did, helping her with her chair. "I understand, Miz Dorsette. You've got your work cut out for you."

"And so do you, son." She glanced at Lorna when she said this, then turned to give Mick a knowing look.

He didn't miss the implications. Hilda Dorsette figured he'd get the job done, if he could just convince her niece to stay out of the way.

He sat back down, hoping to do just that. Glancing from Lacey to Lorna, he said, "So, do you two ladies have any more questions or concerns?"

Lacey smiled over at him. "I don't. I'm sure you know what you're doing. I think the best thing we can do is leave you to your work."

She got up, too, and again Mick did the gentlemanly thing by helping her with her chair. Lacey seemed a tad more centered and serene than her younger sister. Her smile was politeness itself.

"I have to walk down to the shop and make sure what little damage we received falls under the insurance policy."

"What kind of shop do you run?" Mick asked, once again amazed at the Dorsette women. Except for Lorna. He wasn't sure what she did around here, except pray and tell people off in French.

"Antiques," Lacey explained. "The Antique Garden, to be exact. You passed it when you came in through the gate. It used to be the overseer's cottage. We get a lot of business during the tourist season."

"I don't know a thing about antiques," Mick said. "I move around way too much to set up housekeeping."

He didn't miss the way Lorna's eyebrows lifted, or the little smirk of disdain on her pert face. He guessed someone as countrified and dour as Miss Lorna Dorsette didn't cotton to a traveling man too much.

"That's a shame," Lacey replied, her skirts swishing as she went about cleaning the table. "I love old things. They keep me rooted and remind me of where I came from."

Mick didn't need anything around to remind him of where he'd come from. That's why he kept on moving. But these lovely ladies didn't need to hear that particular revelation. He sat silent, well aware that he should just get back to work and forget about trying to impress the Dorsette sisters.

Lacey bid them good morning, and that left…Lorna.

He didn't have to look at her to know she was impatiently tapping a foot underneath the round wrought-iron table. Too much caffeine, he reasoned. And he couldn't resist the grin or the sideways look. "Uh…and what do you do? How do you stay occupied?"

Lorna tossed her long flaming hair over her shoulder, still staring daggers after her ethereal sister. "Oh, not much," she stated as she waved a hand in the air. "I guess you could say I'm the chief cook and bottle washer."

Another surprise. "But I thought Rosie Lee was the cook. And a mighty fine one, at that."

Mick had first met the robust Cajun woman when the trucks had rolled up over two hours ago. Apparently, she and her equally robust husband, Tobbie, helped out around the place. While Rosie Lee had introduced Mick to Emily, their teenage daughter and

Tobias, or Little Tobbie, the youngest of the six Babineaux children, Big Tobbie immediately began assisting Mick's crew in setting up. Then Rosie Lee and Emily had given everyone coffee to get them started, while Little Tobbie had badgered Mick with questions about all the big equipment.

"What's that do?" the black-haired eight-year-old had asked, pointing with a jelly-covered finger to one of the bucket trucks.

"That, my friend, lifts my men up high, so they can get to the trees," Mick had explained.

"Can I have a ride?"

"Hush up," Rosie Lee had told her youngest son. "That little imp will drive you crazy, Mr. Love."

Rosie Lee had jet-black hair which she wore in a long braid down her back, and a jolly personality, which caused her to chuckle over her words. At least *she* was cheerful and down-to-earth. Rosie Lee had given him extra French toast loaded with fresh strawberries. They had bonded instantly.

But Lorna now only gave him a sweet smile that clearly told him he was way out of his league. "Rosie Lee works for me. And she is a very good cook. She and Tobbie, and their entire family for that matter, have been working for us for more than twenty years now. But I do most of the cooking for our guests, and I run the restaurant out back. It was once the carriage house and stables." She stopped, took a sip of coffee. "We had to shut it down, though. The storm damaged part of the roof, and we've got a major leak in one of the dining rooms."

Mick turned to squint into the trees. "Just how many places of business do y'all have around here?"

She actually almost smiled. "The house, the restaurant and the antique shop. Oh, and our brother Lucas has his own business on the side."

"What side would that be?"

She shrugged, causing her hair to move like a golden waterfall at sunset back around her shoulders. "You never know with Lucas. He does a little trapping here, a little singing and saxophone playing there, and a little crop dusting whenever someone calls him, but mostly, he does whatever he pleases, whenever the mood strikes him."

"A trapping, singing, crop-dusting Cajun?" Mick had to laugh. "I'm getting a good picture of your family, Lorna. You pray and stomp. Lacey smiles and flutters. And you just explained Lucas—he likes to play. And I guess Aunt Hilda is the sensible glue that holds all of you together, huh?"

He'd been teasing, but the serious look in her eyes stopped the joke. "Did I say something wrong?"

"No," she replied, shaking her head. "You hit the nail right on the head, especially about Lacey and Lucas, and even me, I guess—although I don't always stomp around. Aunt Hilda *is* the backbone of this family, this entire town. You see, we've lived with her since we were children. After...after our parents died, she took us in."

Mick wasn't grinning anymore. "That's tough, about your parents. I didn't mean to make fun—"

Lorna held up a dainty hand. "It's all right, really."

But he could see that darkness in her eyes, a darkness that took them from bright green to a deep rich shade of sad. And he could also see shards of fear and doubt centered there, too, as if it wasn't really all right at all.

Wanting to say something to replace the foot he'd just extracted from his big mouth, Mick said, "Well, Hilda Dorsette seems like a good woman. And this is certainly a beautiful place."

"Yes, to both," Lorna replied, drumming her fingers on the table again. "Which is why I overreacted earlier. I just hate to see any part of Bayou le Jardin destroyed, and I guess I felt helpless. So I took it all out on you and your men. But, hey, we can't change an act of God, can we."

"No, Mother Nature doesn't discriminate."

"And God always has His reasons, I suppose. Aunt Hilda says we should never question God."

Mick watched as she jumped up—didn't even give him a chance to help her out of her chair. Did she resent God, then, for taking her parents? No, she'd said she prayed to Him. But...maybe even though she believed in God, she still had some harsh thoughts holed up in that pretty head of hers. And since she couldn't take everything out on God, Mick Love would probably come in handy.

He was getting the picture, all right.

And he'd have to tread lightly in order to avoid this cute little woman's wrath. Or he'd have to flirt with her to take her mind off her troubles.

Either way, his time at Bayou le Jardin surely wouldn't be boring. Not one little bit.

"We've still got a little bit of cleaning up to do in the rear gardens," Mick told Lorna hours later, as they stood beneath the remaining live oaks in the backyard. "Then tomorrow we can start on that big one by the back gallery. I'm afraid there's not much to do for that one but cut it down and break up as much of that massive stump as possible. Even your expert landscaper Mr. Hayes agrees with me there."

Lorna placed her hands on her hips, then looked over at the tree that had clipped part of the roof during the storm. The tree looked as if someone had taken its trunk and twisted it around until it had reached the breaking point. "Yes, I suppose if you did try to salvage what's left, it would only be misshapen and mainly a stump with twigs sprouting from it." She shook her head. "That tree has been there for centuries."

"I know," Mick said, taking her by the arm to

guide her around broken limbs and torn roof tiles. "I've always loved trees."

Lorna glanced over at him. He was filthy dirty from stomping around in mud and bushes all day, but he still had an air of authority about him that dirt and sweat couldn't mask. He'd worked side by side with the ten or so men on his crew, issuing orders in a clear, precise way without ever raising his voice or exerting power. She certainly couldn't fault him—he'd done a good job of clearing up the debris.

But he sure could use a shower.

Glad she'd had one herself and even more glad she'd changed into a flowing denim skirt and printed cotton scoop-neck T-shirt, Lorna told herself to stop being silly. It had been a very long time since she'd taken time to dress for a man. She wasn't about to start now. But she had washed her hair, just in case.

Just in case of what?

Wanting to get her mind off Mick Love and back on business, she asked, "Is that why you became a forester, because you like trees?"

Mick shook the dust and dirt out of his tousled hair, then smiled over at her. "Yeah, I guess so. I grew up in rural Mississippi—nothing but trees and kudzu. I used to climb way up high in this great big live oak out in the woods behind our house and pretend I was Tarzan."

Lorna laughed out loud. "Did you swing through the kudzu vines and yell like Tarzan?"

He actually blushed, just a faint tinge of pink against tanned skin and dirt smudges. ''Yeah, and I beat my chest, too.'' Then he demonstrated, his fist hitting his broad chest as he made a strange and rather loud call.

''Hey, boss, stop trying to impress that pretty woman and tell us it's time to call it a day, please.''

Mick and Lorna turned to find Josh Simmons, Mick's assistant and crew foreman, laughing at them from the corner of the house.

Josh stepped forward, his hard hat in his hands, a big grin on his chocolate-colored face. ''Miz Dorsette, that's the only way he knows how to attract females.''

Mick groaned. ''Yeah, and sometimes it only brings out the wrong kind.''

Lorna could understand that. Even pretending to be a savage, Mick Love made her shudder and wonder. He was definitely all male, and every bit as tempting as any Tarzan she'd ever seen at the movies. And he was as tanned and muscular as any outdoorsman she'd ever been around.

Stop it, Lorna, she told herself. Then to bring her simmering heart back under control, she asked, ''Where are you and your crew staying?''

Mick looked surprised. ''Hadn't really thought about that. Is there a hotel around here?''

Lorna scoffed, then waved a hand. ''We *are* a bed-and-breakfast, Mick. Why don't you stay here?'' And wondered immediately why she'd just invited the man to stay at her home.

"But that would be way too much trouble," Mick replied, his blue eyes skimming over her face, her hair. "I don't want to be a bother."

"Nonsense," Lorna exclaimed. "Most of our guests have checked out because of the storm, anyway." Trying to hide the fact that his eyes moving over her made her feel like a delicate flower lifting to find the sun, she turned to Josh, instead. "We have several guest cottages around the bend in the lane. The storm missed them—just some minor repairs. They sleep six to a cottage, so you and your men can take the first two. They're clean and waiting, and they have bathrooms and everything you need to be comfortable. Breakfast is at the main house, and the restaurant should be open again in a day or so. We'll furnish all of your other meals there, free of charge. And if we can't open up again, don't worry. Rosie Lee and I will see to it that you're fed properly."

"We couldn't—"

"Mick, you drove for hours to come here and help us—I insist."

They stood there, staring at each other. Lorna knew she'd just issued more than an invitation for a place to stay. And so did Mick Love. At least, the expectant look in his eyes gave her that impression.

"Well, what's it gonna be, boss?" Josh said, a questioning gaze widening his face. "These fellows are dirty and hungry and about to fall asleep in their boots.''

Mick looked back at the trucks, where the men sat gathered and waiting for his next order. Then he turned back to Lorna. ''Are you sure?''

''Very sure,'' she told him, wishing that were true. Having Mick Love underfoot day and night meant having a big complication in her life. And she didn't need any complications right now. As far as men were concerned, anyway. She'd had enough of those to last a lifetime. But then, she couldn't send the man away. Not after the hard work he'd put in cleaning up the gardens. And there was still lots of work ahead.

''It just makes sense,'' she said aloud, but more to convince herself than Mick. ''How long do you think you'll be here?''

Mick wrinkled his nose, which made him only look more adorable. ''At least a couple of days, maybe all week.''

''Then it's settled. I'll have Rosie Lee get the keys and some fresh towels, and Tobbie can show you to the cottages.''

''Okay,'' Mick said. ''Thank you.''

''Don't mention it. We owe you our own thanks.''

After finding Rosie Lee and telling her what needed to be done, Lorna watched as Mick and his men followed Tobbie to the cottages. She could handle this. She could handle having him around for a couple of days. Soon, this mess would be cleaned up, and he'd be gone, and life would return to normal.

Then Lucas came strolling up, a lopsided grin on his handsome face. "*Chère,* you look tired. Long day?"

Lorna nodded her head, then frowned up at him. "Yes, long day. And where have you been?"

Her brother shrugged, tipped his black curly haired head. "Never you mind. I had things to see about."

Lorna knew she wouldn't get anything more from Lucas. He was either playful or moody, depending on which way the tide was flowing.

She hurried ahead of him. "I want to survey the damage once more before dusk. Since you didn't take the time this morning to see for yourself, you can come with me or not. It doesn't matter to me."

"Little sister isn't pleased with Lucas," he said, his long fingers, touching her on her chin, trying to tickle a smile out of her.

Lorna refused to give in to her brother's charms. She was furious with him for staying away all day. Just like Lucas to slink off and hide from his responsibilities. Or maybe he just couldn't face the natural disaster that had almost destroyed his beloved Bayou le Jardin. He'd been up before any of the rest of them, and gone by sunrise.

Lucas was always full of surprises, so she wouldn't put it past him to have been off helping someone else get through the devastation of the storm, rather than face his own close brush with mortality. Lucas laughed at death, had stood out on the gallery in the wee hours, daring the storm to pass over Bayou le Jardin. And had probably been just as scared and worried as any of them. But he'd never come out and admit that, of course.

Well, this storm had rattled all of them. Lorna offered a prayer for peace and calm. She just wanted things fixed and back to normal. After everything she'd been through leading up to her return to Bayou le Jardin, she now liked "normal."

But then Lucas grabbed her by the hand, his next words really taking her by surprise. "Oh, by the way, I just ran into Mick Love. Seems like a nice enough fellow. I invited him up to the house for supper."

And that's when Lorna Dorsette realized her life might never return to normal again.

Chapter Three

❧

"**I** can't believe Lucas asked the man up here for supper. I was fully prepared to send something down to Mick and the rest of his crew."

Lorna flounced around in the big kitchen, worrying over the thick, dark shrimp-and-sausage gumbo she and Rosie Lee had been preparing all afternoon. After stirring the gumbo yet again, she opened the door of one of the two industrial-sized ovens to make sure her French bread was browning to perfection.

"Will you relax," Lacey told her from her spot across the kitchen. "Lucas probably heard about the ruckus between Mr. Love and you this morning, that's all. Knowing Lucas, he deliberately invited Mick here just to get on your nerves."

Lorna whirled to glare at her sister. Why did Lacey always looked so pulled together, when Lorna felt

like a limp, overcooked noodle? In spite of the cool
night, the spring humidity and the heat from the ovens
was making her sweat like a sugar-cane farmer, while
it only made her older sister glisten like a lady.

Blowing hair off her face, she said, "Well, *you're
all* getting on my nerves. You with your smirks and
teasing remarks, Lucas with his shenanigans—and
now I've got to sit through supper with Mick Love
hovering around. I just want to curl up with a good
book and then sleep for twelve hours, but I've got the
restaurant repairs to worry about and a million other
things to keep me awake." *Never mind Mick Love,*
she thought to herself.

Lacey finished putting ice in the tall goblets Rosie
Lee had lined up on a serving cart, then turned to her
sister. "Well, you can prove Lucas wrong, you know.
He just likes to shake things up, then sit back and
watch the fireworks. So, don't give him anything to
watch."

Lorna lifted her chin a notch. "You might be right
there. If I act like a perfect lady, using the impeccable
manners Aunt Hilda instilled in all of us, then Lucas
will be sorely disappointed and Mick Love will be
put in his place."

"And just what is his place?" Lacey said, lifting
her perfectly arched brows. "I think Lucas is right, if
he did figure this out. I think Mick Love gets to you."

"Don't be a dolt," Lorna retorted. "I simply meant

that Mick Love is here to do a job, and that should be that.''

"You'd think.''

"And what's that supposed to mean?''

"If the man has no effect on you, why are you so nervous? You're jumping around like a barn cat.''

"I'm perfectly fine,'' Lorna retorted again. "And if everyone around here would just mind their own business—''

"Have we ever?'' Lacey shot her a tranquil smile, then took the tea tray. Pushing through the swinging door from the kitchen to the formal dining room, she called over her shoulder. "Better take a deep breath, sister. Mr. Love just walked in the back door.''

"Easy for you to say,'' Lorna mumbled, after her sister was well out of earshot. "Nothing ever ruffles your feathers. Smooth as glass, calm as a backwater bayou. That's our Lacey.''

She'd often wondered how her sister got away with it. Lacey held it all together, no matter what. She was the oldest, had witnessed the death of their parents. Lacey had saved Lucas and Lorna from a similar fate by hiding them away, but none of them ever talked about that. Ever.

Especially Lacey. She kept it all inside, hidden beneath that calm countenance. And she'd done the same thing when she'd become a widow at an early age, and through all the other tragedies in her life since. She'd even remained calm during the thrashing of the storm, never once moaning or whining or worrying.

Lacey had herded the few terrified guests—an older couple staying in the downstairs blue bedroom and a set of newlyweds staying in the honeymoon suite on the second floor—down into the kitchen root cellar along with the family, soothing them with soft words all the while, telling them not to worry.

Lorna had done enough of that for all of them, she supposed. But she hadn't whined aloud. She'd pleaded and prayed with God to spare her home and guests, to spare her town, from any death or destruction brought on by the wailing tornado bearing down on them.

Even now, she could hear the wind moaning, grinding around the house.... Wind that only reminded her of that other night so long ago.

"Hey, need any help here?"

Lorna pivoted so fast, she knocked a wooden spoon off the counter. She turned to find Mick standing there in clean jeans and a faded red polo shirt, a lopsided smile on his interesting, little-boy face.

He pushed still-wet hair off his forehead. "Guess I shoulda knocked."

Lorna held up a hand, willing it not to shake. "It's okay. You just startled me. I was thinking about the storm and remembering—"

He was across the spacious room in three long strides. "Are you sure you're all right?"

Anger at her brother for putting her in the position of polite hostess, and a need to find control, brought Lorna out of her stupor. "I'm fine. It was just...so scary. I was concerned for our guests, of course. I'm not really afraid of the weather—they say the weather in Louisiana changes every thirty minutes and that does hold some truth—but this storm was different. It was so powerful, so all-consuming. And I just keep remembering—"

She just kept remembering another night, another dark, storm-tossed night long ago. A night she had buried in that secret place in her mind and soul. Was she confusing the two?

"I just can't get it out of my mind," she said, completely unaware that she'd spoken.

Until Mick took her trembling hand in his. "You survived a major catastrophe, Lorna. It's understandable that you might have some sort of post-traumatic reaction."

She had to laugh at that. Placing a hand over her mouth, she tried to stifle the giggles. Sometimes, she thought her whole life since her parents' death had been one big post-traumatic reaction.

Mick looked down at her as if she'd lost her senses. And she supposed she did look quite mad laughing at his very serious observation. "I'm sorry," she said, sobering and becoming quiet. And becoming so very aware of the man standing in front of her. He sure cleaned up nicely. And smelled like a fresh forest after a gentle rain.

To make amends for acting like an idiot, she said, "It's just been a rather long day, and I'm exhausted. We've had to cancel guest reservations for the weekend and send others away. None of us has had any rest since the storm hit, and it's only going to continue until we get this place cleaned up and open to the public again."

He guided her to a nearby high-backed chair, gently pushing her down on the thickly hewn straw bottom. "And it's understandable if you don't feel up to having company for dinner."

He rose to leave, but Lorna's hand on his arm stopped him. "No, stay." Then she jumped up, rushing past him to check on the bread. "I mean, we've set a place for you and Aunt Hilda is looking forward to talking with you. You can't leave now."

He leaned on the long wooden counter in the middle of the room, then looked at her in a way that left her senses reeling, in a way that made her think he could easily read her deepest secrets. Then he smiled again. "I guess that would be rude."

"Yes, it would. Just ignore me. I'm all right, really." Pushing at his arm, she said, "Why don't you go into the front parlor with Aunt Hilda and Lacey. I think my brother Lucas is there, too. I'll be out just as soon as I cut the bread."

"And you'll be okay?"

Lorna ignored the little spot in her heart that longed to shout for help, for someone to soothe all the pain and make her feel better. She didn't need, didn't want, pity or sympathy. And she couldn't bring herself to ask for comfort.

"I'm a big girl, Mick. I think I can manage through supper." She pointed a finger toward the swinging door. "But if you could tell Rosie Lee I'm ready to serve now…"

"Sure," Mick said, backing toward the door. "I saw her and Tobbie in the dining room. I'll get her for you."

"Thank you." Lorna watched him leave, then turned to the stove, letting out a long breath that she hadn't even realized she'd been holding.

She didn't understand why being around Mick seemed to turn her into a bubbling, blathering mess. She'd been in charge of her senses early this morning, even when he'd landed smack on top of her. Even when he'd saved her from that tree limb.

Saved her.

Lorna saw her distorted reflection in one of the wide, paned kitchen windows, and knew instantly what was the matter with her.

Mick had saved her life, or had, at least, thrown himself between her and danger. These strange, erratic stirrings deep inside her were only gut reactions to what he'd done. She felt gratitude toward him, and she didn't know how to express that gratitude.

"That's all it is," she told herself. "The man protected me from that giant oak limb." *And I didn't even bother to thank him.*

A voice rang as clear as a dinner bell inside her head. *And maybe...Mick Love saved you from yourself.*

It had been a long, long time since Lorna had allowed anyone else to be her protector. She'd never accepted that she needed rescuing, had never allowed anyone other than her immediate family close enough to see her fear. But because of what could have been a freak accident, because she'd been in the wrong place at the wrong time, Mick had gotten way too close.

Had he seen her fear? Was that why he seemed so solicitous of her? Was that why she felt so vulnerable around him?

"Leave it to me to do a foolish thing like stand underneath a broken limb." But then, she reminded herself, she always somehow managed to be in the wrong place when things turned from bad to worse.

Or maybe she'd been in the *right* place at the *right* time. Aunt Hilda always said God put people in certain circumstances to get them where they needed to be.

And Lorna had been in that place at that time, praying for something, someone to help her understand. She'd told Mick that God had answered her prayers by sending him. That much was the truth, at least. He'd come along exactly when she needed him.

That was a debt Lorna wasn't ready to accept or repay. Yet somehow, she knew she'd have to find a way to do just that.

Mick found Rosie Lee and Tobbie Babineaux busily setting up the dining room, little Tobias at their feet playing with a hand-held computer game. Mick watched as the couple laughed and worked together, side by side. He envied their easy banter and loving closeness. They were married with six children, yet the radiant smiles on their faces showed how much they enjoyed being together.

"Hello," he said as he strolled toward them, then touched a hand to Little Tobbie's arm in greeting. "You folks need any help?"

"Mr. Love," Rosie Lee said, laughing so hard her whole belly shook, "you the guest. We the workers."

Mick shrugged and laughed right along with her. He liked her strong Cajun accent. "Sorry. I'm just used to earning my keep."

Tobias immediately jumped up. "I saw you up in a tree. Don't you get scared, being way up high like that?"

"Nope," Mick replied, leaning over to ruffle the boy's shining black hair. "I'm so used to it, I don't even think about it."

Tobias's black eyes burned with questions. "I can

climb way up high, too. Maybe I can be a tree man one day.''

His mother groaned, then turned to her son. ''You stay out of Mr. Love's way, you hear? Don't go climbing any more trees, either. You almost got stuck the other day, remember?''

''I need me one of them buckets like Mr. Mick uses, I guess.'' Tobias grinned, then scooted away before his mother could grab him.

''I'm going out back to play,'' he called, already running out the open door.

''Don't bother Mr. Love's equipment,'' his father warned.

Mick grinned, then turned to Tobbie. ''I bet he's a handful.''

''Yep. And his older brothers just make it worse by teaching him their bad ways, too. Our house is always full of fightin' boys.''

''And a couple of quiet girls,'' his wife said with a grin and a nod.

Mick glanced around the beautiful room. ''Sure is quiet around here tonight.''

Tobbie winked at him. ''All the other guests gone and checked out. Storm got to 'em. So we gonna treat you like royalty—you and your men, that is.''

''Nah, now,'' Mick replied, holding up a hand. ''I'm just a regular joe—no prince. But I have to admit, I could get used to this. This place is amazing.''

Just like the women who run it, he thought to himself. Especially the woman now alone in the kitchen. The woman who didn't want him to see that she was still frightened as a result of the tornado.

But what else was scaring Lorna? He thought about asking Tobbie what had happened to Lorna's parents, but footsteps from the front of the house halted him.

"Hey, man, c'mon up here to the parlor," Lucas called from the wide central hallway, his cowboy boots clicking on the hardwood floors as he walked toward Mick.

"Coming," Mick said, lifting a hand to Rosie Lee and Tobbie. "Oh, Lorna's ready to serve now," he remembered to tell them.

Lucas had an accent similar to theirs, but a bit more cultured. Yet he seemed every bit as Cajun as the Babineaux, while his sisters seemed more refined and pure Southern. But then, this family was as mysterious and full of contrasts as the swamp down below the back gardens.

Maybe if he made small talk with her family, Mick would be able to get a handle on Lorna. He didn't yet understand why she brought out all his protective instincts, or why she fought so hard to hide behind that wall of control. He reckoned it had something to do with him falling headlong into her out there beneath the great oaks this morning.

Saving someone from near death did have a dramatic effect on a person. Didn't that mean he had to protect her for life now? Or was that the other way around? Did she now owe him something in return? That option was certainly worth exploring.

"How ya doing?" Lucas asked, as Mick approached him. "Want some mint iced tea or a cup of coffee? We've even got some kind of fancy mineral water—Lorna insists on keeping it for our guests."

"I'm fine," Mick replied, his gaze sweeping across the winding marble staircase. "Hey, this house is unbelievable."

"Nearly as old as the dirt it's sitting upon," Lucas replied, his grin showing a row of gleaming white teeth, his dark eyes shifting to a deep rich brown as the light hit them. "Been here for well over a hundred and fifty years, at least." He shrugged. "My sisters are the experts on the history of this old house. Me, I prefer hanging out in the swamps where the real history is found."

That statement intrigued Mick. "I bet you've seen some stuff out there."

Lucas nodded, then, with a sweeping gesture, announced Mick to his aunt and sister. "Mr. Mick Love, ladies." Then he turned back to Mick. "The swamp holds all of her secrets close, but I've seen a few of her treasures and a few of her dangers, yeah."

Mick thought that best described Lucas's sister, too. Lorna obviously held her secrets close. But Mick had seen something deep and dark and mysterious there in her green eyes. Something he wanted to explore and expose, bring out into the open. Which might prove to be dangerous, too. He worked too many long hours to even think about getting involved with a redheaded woman.

Glancing around the long parlor, he was once again assaulted by the opulence and old-world elegance of Bayou le Jardin. His gaze swept the fireplace, then settled on a small portrait of a dark-haired man and a beautiful woman with strawberry-blond hair, centered over the mantel.

"Our parents," Lucas told him in a low voice, his black eyes as unreadable as a moonless night. "They died when we were children."

Mick wanted to ask Lucas what had happened, but on seeing the look on the other man's face he decided that might not be such a good idea. Mick had lots of questions, for lots of reasons he couldn't even begin to understand or explain.

Right now, though, he had to remember his manners and make polite conversation with the Dorsette bunch. And wonder all the while why he was so attracted to Lorna.

"That was one of the best meals I've had in a very long time," Mick told Lorna later, as they all sat around the long mahogany dining table. "I don't get much home cooking."

"Oh, and why is that?" Aunt Hilda asked. She sat, stirring rich cream into her coffee, a bowl of bread pudding on her dessert plate. "And while we're talking, where did you grow up? Who's your family?"

Mick glanced around the table. Everything about Bayou le Jardin was elegant and cultured, down to the silverware and lace-edged linen napkins. And he was sure the lineage went back centuries, too. Aunt Hilda's question was typical of blue-blooded rich people. They didn't really care about you; they just wanted to make sure you came from good Southern stock. He didn't begrudge her the question, but he did find it pointed and obvious, and amusing. She wanted to know if she could trust him, count on him to do what was right.

Did he really want to tell these people that he'd grown up in a trailer park deep in the Mississippi Delta with an abusive father? Or should he just tell them that after his old man had drunk himself to death, his mother had changed from a weak, submissive wife into a strong, determined woman who wanted the best for her only son? Should he tell them she'd worked two jobs just to make sure Mick finished school and learned a trade? Or that she had died from a heart attack before she could enjoy his success? Should he tell them that he had no one to go home to, now that she was dead? And that the woman he'd planned on marrying had dumped him for someone else? That he'd left the Delta and had never looked back?

Mick looked at Lorna, saw the questioning lift of

her arched brows, and knew he wasn't nearly good enough to be sitting at this table. So he simply said, "I was born and raised in Mississippi, and I still have a home there right outside of Vicksburg—that is, when I can ever get back to it."

"So you travel around a lot." This statement came from Lorna. She'd obviously already summed him up.

Mick glanced over at her without bothering to defend himself. She sat there, bathed in golden light from the multifaceted chandelier hanging over the table, her hands in her lap, her hair falling in ringlets of satin fire around her face and down her back. She was beautiful in a different kind of way. Not classic, but fiery and defiant. Mick couldn't explain it, but he could certainly see that beauty. And feel it. It washed over him like a golden rain, leaving him unsteady and unsure.

Wanting to give her a good answer, he went for the truth this time. "Yeah, we stay on the road a lot. We travel all over the state, and on rare occasions, such as this, we travel out of state. Do a lot of work in Alabama and Georgia, too. I reckon you could say we go wherever the work takes us."

"You probably keep steady," Lucas said, before taking a long swig of his tea. "There's always trees around."

"If you have your way, that is," Lacey interjected. "Lucas is a naturalist—the protector of the bayou."

She grinned, but Mick didn't miss the pride in her eyes.

"Among my many other talents," Lucas said, his dark eyes twinkling with merriment.

"Yes, and if we could just pinpoint what exactly you *are* good at and make you stick with it, we might all be able to retire with a nice nest egg," Lorna stated, her attention now on her brother.

Lucas pumped up his chest. "Now, suga', you know I'm good at whatever I set my mind to."

His sisters and aunt all laughed, then shook their heads. Soon, they were all talking at once, each giving pointed suggestions as to what Lucas needed to do with his sorry life.

Mick was just glad the conversation had switched away from him. Even if Lorna's gaze did drift back to him now and again.

Then Lucas made an intriguing remark. "Well, sister, you're a fine one to ask Mr. Love about traveling." He grinned toward Mick. "Lorna took off a few years back, traveled all over the world, settled in Paris for a while."

"I went to cooking school," Lorna snapped as she stared hard at her brother.

"And now she runs a French restaurant out back and cooks good old Cajun, Creole and American food for the houseguests," Lacey explained with pride.

"She's a bona fide chef," Lucas replied with a wink.

Mick raised his tea goblet toward her in a salute. So she wasn't just a country bumpkin, all tucked away here on the bayou. He wondered why he'd even thought that. Lorna was as sophisticated as any French woman, and she could definitely speak the language—very colorfully. Lifting his glass high, he said, "And I thought all the great chefs were men."

"No, men just like to believe that," she replied, her expression smug.

Mick decided there was probably much more to her travels, but he didn't press for the details. Yet.

When they'd finished their dessert, Lorna, Lacey and Lucas all helped with the dishes, while Aunt Hilda went up to bed on the third floor where their living quarters were located. Rosie Lee and Tobbie had eaten in the kitchen with Emily and Tobias. Emily also worked at Bayou le Jardin, but now they all chipped in to get the work done. Mick was amazed at the sense of family here, and the way the Dorsettes seemed to think of the Babineaux family as part of their own, even down to Little Tobbie running and playing throughout the vast mansion.

He'd never had that. He'd always been an outsider.

And soon, he'd be gone from Bayou le Jardin. Gone from the mystery and secrets of the swamp. Gone from the scent of azalea blossoms and wisteria sprigs on the night wind. Gone from the green-velvet gaze of a red-haired woman with a heart full of fire and a soul full of secrets.

Mick liked traveling around, liked being on the road. Liked running, always running from his past. But tonight, tonight, he felt a stirring that was as unfamiliar to him as crystal goblets and crisp linen napkins, as unfamiliar to him as polished wood and freshly cut flowers.

For the first time since he'd left that trailer park, Mick Love wanted to stay right where he was. Just for a little while.

Just long enough to find out all the secrets Lorna Dorsette kept hidden so well behind all that feminine fire.

He waited until everyone else had bid him goodnight, then he turned to Lorna. They stood on the back gallery, where the moonlight played hide-and-seek with the Spanish moss in the great oaks, where the wisteria blossoms entwined around the stout gallery columns, showering them with delicate purple rain every time the wind lifted.

He didn't want to be away from her just yet.

"Show me the river," he said, reaching out a hand to her as he stepped out into the shadows of the damaged garden.

He watched as moonbeams hit her face, watched as tiny violet-colored wisteria flowers caught and held to her long hair. And again, he saw that distant, disturbing fear in her eyes.

But she took his hand and followed him.

Chapter Four

The big trees cast mushroom-shaped shadows in the moonlight. Lorna walked with Mick through the long front gardens, following the path she'd taken so many times over the years. The dirt and gravel lane was now littered with broken branches and split tree limbs. Thank goodness the storm hadn't taken any of the ancient oak trees completely down. With Mick's help, and their own landscaper, they should be able to re-shape those that had been damaged.

Lorna shuddered in spite of the mild spring night. She should have gone in to get her flashlight. Or better yet, she should have stayed inside tidying up the kitchen, making sure everything was set for breakfast. But then, she reminded herself, all the guests had checked out due to the storm, and she was turning away any reservations until things were back in tiptop shape. It was going to be a long week.

"You okay?" Mick asked. His words echoed over the silent countryside.

Lorna wouldn't tell him that she never came out here at night. That she never walked around the grounds alone at night, or that she always, always carried her powerful flashlight, even when someone was with her.

She took a deep breath. "Fine. Just tired. We're almost there."

The river was across the narrow country road, behind a dirt-and-grass levee that cows grazed on now and then. At this time of year, red clover bloomed profusely along the levee. Lorna could see the clover dancing in the moonlight. It looked like a flowing red scarf winding around the river.

Not wanting Mick to see her apprehension, she held tightly to his hand as he guided her over the cluttered pathway. She managed to let him go long enough to open the black wrought-iron gate that kept uninvited curiosity seekers away from the secluded mansion.

"Looks like the storm clouds are all gone," Mick said, as their footfalls sounded on the paved road.

"Yes, but the levee will be muddy still. So watch your step."

With a spurt of determination, Lorna pushed up the soft loam of the levee to distance herself from Mick, then stood on the crest to stare down at the black, swirling waters of the Mississippi River. "Maybe the spring rains will hold off for a while now. The river is just about overflowing as it is."

Lorna had never realized how beautiful the river was at night. The soft gurgling sound of the tide sang a timeless song, while the buzz of mosquitoes hummed in perfect harmony. She could see fireflies lifting all around them, their flickering iridescent greenish glows like tiny lanterns in the dark.

Which only reminded her that she did not have her own lantern. But she held the panic at bay, determined not to show Mick her humiliating weakness.

Instead, she watched gladly as he trudged up the small incline, right behind her. He stood there a minute with his hands on his hips, then lifted his head to the sky. His silhouette was highlighted by grayish-blue moonlight, casting him in a dreamlike state.

Maybe she was dreaming. She still couldn't understand why she'd taken Mick's hand and allowed him to guide her out into the darkness. She'd only met this man early this morning, under the strangest circumstances, and now she'd walked through the moonlight with him. It had been a while since she'd been alone with a man. And she'd never brought anyone other than family out here to the river—and even then only in broad daylight. Usually their guests wandered around on their own, leaving Lorna to do her work.

What's wrong with me? she wondered now as she

watched Mick through the veil of moonlight and shadows.

Her emotions were raw from the storm, her nerves were like stretched, tangled wires curling tightly through her body, and yet, for some obscure reason, she almost felt safe with Mick Love.

Even in the dark.

"Listen to the water," he said, his head down. "All that undercurrent, all that power. I've always been fascinated by nature."

"Is that why you decided to become a tree expert?"

"Probably. As I told you earlier, I loved getting lost in the woods when I was a child. There wasn't much else to do around the house, so I'd take off for hours on end, just roaming around, exploring, playing make-believe."

Lorna could understand that. "When we first came here, I did the same thing. Lacey and I would wander around the house, pretending we were princesses lost in a castle. When I saw this house and the land surrounding it, I thought I'd found a secret garden. It looked like something out of a fairy tale."

Mick turned then, to look back at the big house looming in the distance. "It's a beautiful spot."

"A safe haven," she replied without thinking.

The image of the great house glowing with yellow lights beckoned her, reminding her that she *was* safe here. It was an image that caused motorists to slow down and stop, inspired artists to keep painting, enticed photographers to take one more picture. From the narrow road, the house came into view around a winding curve, always catching admirers by surprise.

Lorna still slowed down herself to glance over at the panoramic view of the square, pink-walled house with the massive white columns sitting back behind the oak-lined driveway. And it still took her breath away.

"It's home," she said, a great well of love and gratitude pooling in her heart and bringing tears to her eyes. Once again, she thanked God that her home and family had been spared from the worst of the storm.

"How old were you when..." Mick paused, glanced down at the ground.

"When my parents were—when they died?" She had to close her eyes a minute. She still couldn't bring herself to say the word *murdered*. "I was six."

He turned to her, coming much too close. "That must have been tough."

"It was hard." She nodded, wrapped her arms across her midsection to hold off the night chill—and his nearness. Then she glanced back at the house, suddenly very sure that she needed to be back inside, near the warmth of her family, near the lights. "We'd better get back." She hoped he didn't hear the panic in her words.

Mick's expression wasn't hard to read, even in the

grayish night. Confusion, coupled with concern. She'd certainly seen that look before.

"We just got here," he said through a flash of a smile. "But...I can't really see much of the view in the dark, anyway." He leaned closer still. "Except your pretty green eyes, of course."

The flirtation brought Lorna out of her panic. "Did you bring me out here to the river to tell me that?"

He tipped his head to one side, sighed long and hard. "Actually, I don't know why I brought you out here. It was just such a beautiful night, and I felt like going for a walk. I like to walk."

"Me, too, but not at night."

Confusion again—but thankfully, he didn't ask for an explanation.

"And obviously not with someone you barely know."

"I'm fine with that—with you, I mean. Just...don't try anything."

He must have sensed her apprehension, but he didn't comment for a minute or so. He simply stood there, staring down at her. Then he said, "We can go back if you feel uncomfortable with me."

Lorna did feel uncomfortable with him, simply because he made her feel close to being...comfortable. That was almost as unnerving as being out here in the darkness. She was torn between the urge to enjoy the safety of his nearness and the urge to ignore that feeling and run toward home. But she couldn't explain that to him. So she tried to make excuses.

"I'm sorry. I'm so tired, and I've got to get up early to talk to the insurance adjusters and contractors about the restaurant repairs."

"Sure." He reached out to take her hand, tugging her arms away from her body. "I'm sorry, too. I wasn't thinking, dragging you out here." Then he pointed toward the house. "Which room is yours?"

Surprised, Lorna stood silent for a minute. Then she told him. "It's on our far left, on the rear side of the house near where the tree clipped the roof. I have a view of the entire back gardens and the restaurant."

"Do you ever come out on the gallery, to look at the stars?"

Such odd questions. "Sometimes," she responded. *Sometimes, when I get up the courage.*

"Maybe I'll see you up there one night, then." He pulled her down the damp levee. "Thanks for the walk. I needed it after that meal."

"It was nice to just relax a bit," she responded, knowing that she wasn't at all relaxed. "You and your men missed the worst of it—yesterday morning was total chaos. People wandering around, looking for pets, checking on relatives, digging through rubble for what was left of their homes. After we'd assessed the damage here and made sure all our guests were safe, we all went into town to help out there. It's going to take a while to get things cleaned up, but thankfully no one was killed.''

She didn't mention that she'd always remember the roaring rage of the tornado. She'd always remember the agony of being in total darkness while monstrous winds and pelting rains assaulted her home. She couldn't tell him that Lacey had held her hand, that Lucas had touched his fingers to her face there in the pantry, as they'd all three surrounded Aunt Hilda like a protective shield. She couldn't tell him that her worst memories had been trapped inside the silent scream that echoed in her mind over the roar of the storm.

They were alive; they had survived. She had to be thankful that her family had been spared. She had to calm the scream down again and regain control.

This innate fear she had tried so long to bury, this fear that the storm had brought hurtling back to the surface, was clouding her judgment. That had to be why she didn't want to let Mick out of her sight.

''Well, I'll do my part to help y'all out, I promise,'' Mick said, as they strolled back up the drive toward the house. ''We can take a couple of extra days—the men won't mind one bit.''

''Thank you,'' Lorna said, meaning it. She stopped just as they reached the back of the house. A beckoning light glowed from the wide foyer, but she held off a bit longer. ''Mick, I didn't thank you—for saving me from that tree limb this morning.''

"No thanks needed."

Lorna looked out at the back driveway, where the big trucks and heavy equipment had been neatly parked in a long row. Mick was organized to a fault; she'd give him that.

"Yes, I do need to thank you. It was rude of me not to, and even more rude of me to fuss at you and your men. I was just overreacting to the storm, I think."

"I understand," he said. "You don't have to explain."

"You probably get a lot of that, right?" Which was why he was being so gentlemanly and concerned, showing her extra attention, she reasoned.

He grinned, his white teeth gleaming like polished ivory in the moonlight. "Yeah, but never in French. I declare, I think I liked it."

"Oh, you haven't heard my best—I know a few choice phrases of Cajun French, too. Lucas taught me."

"About Lucas—he does seem a lot more Cajun than the rest of you. Why's that?"

Lorna shrugged. "When we first came here, Lucas was nine years old. For some reason, he immediately bonded with the Babineaux family. Since then, he's spent more time with them than he has with the rest of us. He's picked up their ways, which I guess is natural. Our father was Cajun and our mother was

French-Irish. Lucas looks just like our father, and Lacey and I resemble our mother.''

"Your mother must have been beautiful, then."

Lorna's heart lifted like the delicate wisteria vine
on a nearby railing, taken by an unexpected wind.
"She was very pretty, as you probably could tell if
you saw the portrait over the fireplace in the parlor.
Lacey looks more like her than I do. And acts just
like her, too."

"You and Lacey are both attractive women."

"How kind of you to say that."

She wanted to ask him which he found more attractive, but stubborn pride made her keep the burning
question to herself. It didn't matter anyway, did it?
Anyone could look at Lacey and see a pure lady.
While it was obvious Lorna was a hopeless cause—
half tomboy, half wild child.

"I wasn't being kind. You are a pretty woman,
Lorna."

He stood there again, silent and staring. The man
certainly didn't mind taking in his fill. Lorna tried not
to fidget, but she wasn't used to this kind of attention
from a good-looking stranger.

"Thank you," she managed to say, remembering
how Aunt Hilda had taught her to accept a compli-
ment with graciousness, not excuses and self-
incriminating remarks. Yet Lorna found herself wanting to correct Mick. He didn't know her—couldn't
understand that she doubted his sincerity.

He must have sensed her discomfort, though—yet again.

"Well, thanks for the tour. Good night, Lorna."

He turned to walk down the path leading to the cottages, his sturdy boots pushing at more broken branches.

"Good night. See you in the morning."

He waved, then headed off into the darkness.

Lorna watched him disappear from sight, then hurried inside to the welcoming light.

Mick went into the tiny cottage bedroom he was sharing with Josh Simmons and one of the other workers, the rookie named David. The kid was already sacked out in one of the small beds, his snores of contentment echoing through the cozy sitting room where Josh was relaxing in front of the small television, listening to the evening news on low.

Josh grinned then held a finger to his lips as Mick came into the room. "Boss, you wore that boy slap out."

"He'll get used to it," Mick said, settling down in one of the dainty armchairs to smile at his friend. "But he'll sure be sore come morning."

Josh rubbed his own neck. "Yep, I'm aching myself. But we put in a good day's work."

"With more to come tomorrow," Mick replied. "Did y'all get enough to eat?"

Josh moaned, then patted his flat belly. "Way too much. That Lorna and Rosie Lee, they can sure put on a spread. We ate out on one of the picnic tables—it was turned over from the storm, but we set it right."

Mick could just see Josh issuing directions. "It was nice of them to give us supper."

Josh grinned again. "And how was it up at the big house?"

Mick knew that teasing look. Josh was a real ladies' man himself, so he liked to watch when one of the other fellows got involved in a relationship. Mick needed to set his well-meaning friend straight, though.

"The food was great, the conversation sparkling in spite of all the talk about the storm. What else can I say?"

"And how was Miss Lorna Dorsette?"

Mick gave up. He couldn't lie to his friend. He rubbed a hand down the beard stubble covering his face. "She was just fine. We went for a nice walk by the river, but she did seem a bit skittish."

"Whoa, you're moving right along on this one," Josh said, throwing an embroidered sofa pillow at his boss. "No wonder the woman is skittish—she's having a really strange week, and now you come along."

Mick attempted to keep a straight face. "Hold on, now. I'm just being nice to a lady. We both know we don't get much of a chance to be around ladies in our line of work."

"No, more like old married women who want to boss us around and blame us for their dead trees and equally dead marriages."

"You sound bitter, my friend."

"Just smart. Single women don't seem to need trees cut down or stumps removed, know what I mean? They're out having fun, without us."

"Poor thing," Mick replied, throwing the pillow back at Josh. "You know, marriage and settling down aren't such bad things."

Josh raised a dark eyebrow. "Yeah, I know that— but this coming from a man who's said time and time again he'd never get hitched? Did a tree limb fall on your head, boss, or did saving the lovely Miss Lorna make you change your tune?"

"Maybe both," Mick admitted, grinning sheepishly. "No, I just mean that we're both put off about marriage because we've seen the bad side of things. My dad and his drinking, my breakup with Melinda. You and your brothers and sisters being moved from pillar to post—"

"'Cause my momma couldn't provide for us on her own," Josh finished. "Yeah, man, and we need to remember where we come from. And we need to keep the faith, as my dear momma would say." He waved a hand in the air. "This place is like something out of *Lifestyles of the Rich and Famous.* Not for the likes of you and me."

"Yeah, you're probably right, there," Mick replied. "I'm going to bed."

Josh got up, too. "Hey, man, I didn't mean to tell you what to do. Lorna is sure pretty, and we all could tell the sparks were flying out there between you two. I'd just hate to see you get in over your head."

"I get you," Mick said, nodding. "I'm just trying to help her—all of them—through a rough time. They seem like good people." He turned at the open door to the other small bedroom off the sitting room. "That's why I've been thinking I might stay on here a couple of extra days—send you and the men back to Vicksburg once we've cleared up the worst of it."

Josh's eyes opened wide. "Am I hearing right? Mick Love wants to stay in one spot longer than a day or two?" Then he raised a finger toward his friend. "Man, you got it bad. Go on now, admit it. You want to hang around here, and it ain't got nothin' to do with landscaping or clearing trees."

Mick let out a groan. "Okay, but if I promise to be a good boy and mind my manners, will you let me have some much-needed comp time?"

Josh nodded his head. "Boss, you can have all the comp time you want. You deserve a vacation—never knew you to even take one. Just be careful."

"I intend to," Mick answered. "Just doing my good deed for the week, Josh."

"Yeah, right." Josh brushed past him, still grinning. "I'm turning in. Hey, don't forget to say your prayers."

The lighthearted comment was just another reminder of Josh's firm faith. Even though he'd grown up in a large, poor family, his mother had always managed to get all her children to church each Sunday. Sometimes Mick thought Josh's gentle nudging was the only thing that kept him attending off and on through the years. Josh had enough faith for the both of them.

"I'll be there in a minute," Mick told him. "And I want the left bunk, okay?"

"Why, so you can stare out the window at that mansion up on the hill?"

Mick chuckled. "Yeah, something like that."

About a half-hour later, Mick was stretched out on the crisp white sheets of the old-fashioned brass bed, the window by his left side open to the fragrant night air.

And open to Lorna's bedroom directly across the garden and way up high on the third floor.

He lay there, staring up at that lighted window, wondering why Lorna Dorsette had gotten to him when so many other women had never been able to get near. Not even the woman he'd pledged to marry once, long ago.

Maybe it had been Lorna's green eyes, surprised and luminous, staring up at him when he'd pulled her away from that falling limb out in the garden. Or maybe it had been all that long red-blond hair toppling out of that ridiculous baseball cap. Or maybe it was just a physical attraction, plain and simple.

But no, there was something more, something he sensed there in the depths of her eyes. At times, she seemed almost like a little girl, her eyes full of fear.

She tried hard to hide it behind all that polished control, but it was there.

And it made Mick want to get to know her, to protect her, to touch her. And not just physically. He wanted to see inside her, touch her heart.

"I'm getting downright sappy," he whispered to the darkness.

He thought about the long day—thought about Lorna and her family, devout in their faith, loyal in their sense of family and community. Those were things he'd never had, had tried to avoid all his adult life. Things that he didn't think he was anywhere near worthy enough to receive.

Now he found himself turning toward that single glowing light, wondering what it would be like to have faith in something, someone. Wondering what it would be like to be part of a big, loving family. That light beckoned him, called to him, as it flowed out into the night from atop a mansion Mick had no business dreaming about.

From the bedroom of a woman he surely had no business thinking about.

And yet, he did.

Sometime before dawn, he awoke and turned to look up through the trees, searching for Lorna's room there in the darkness.

He was surprised to see that her bedroom light was still on. Over the coming days, he'd discover that the light stayed on all through the night, always.

Chapter Five

~~

Lorna stood surveying the damaged roof of the Garden Restaurant. The noise of beams being ripped from the ceiling only accented the memories being ripped from her heart.

Her three years of being back here at Bayou le Jardin had been filled with good memories. Peaceful memories. Quiet memories. She wanted to get that back. She didn't want the bad memories to take over again.

Turning to Lacey, she let out a long sigh. "I can't let this storm interrupt my life any longer. I sure hope the contractors can get this repaired in a couple of days."

Lacey placed a hand on her sister's arm. "Lorna, relax. They're working on the roof, and the rest of the damage is not that bad. Didn't they tell you they'd work 'round the clock to fix it?''

"Yes, they did. But I'm losing business and money. Not to mention having to deal with the insurance people."

Lacey nodded her understanding. "Why don't you leave this to the workers and come into town with me. We're taking sandwiches to help out the Red Cross."

"I know that," Lorna snapped, irritation at her sister making her harsh. "I helped fix the sandwiches early this morning."

"Then why don't you stop thinking about yourself and come with us to help the other people—the ones who don't even have a house to go back to?"

Lorna looked at her sister, then realized she was being a bit selfish. "Listen to me—whining as if I'm the only person in the world who's been affected by the tornado. Okay, I'll go with you. I guess this little problem *is* minor compared to what others have been going through."

"Precisely," Lacey agreed. "I know you're worried, Lorna. But we'll be okay."

"How's Aunt Hilda holding up?" Lorna asked, forcing herself to turn away from the construction work, only to be assaulted by the grind of chain saws and wood-mulching machines on the other side of the garden. "She seemed tired last night."

"She's exhausted," Lacey replied, as they headed

back toward the mansion. "But she insists she has to be right there in the thick of the cleanup operations."

"The way I feel I need to be right here with my restaurant?"

Lacey grinned, lifting her voice over the roar of machinery. "Yes. I guess we are a stubborn, pushy lot, huh?"

"Don't I know it." Lorna glanced around as workers in hard hats moved hurriedly here and there. She automatically searched for Mick, then chided herself for doing so.

She hadn't seen him at breakfast, which had been almost a relief after last night. She hadn't slept very well, knowing he was down there in the cottage, knowing that he now knew where her bedroom was, that he hoped she'd come out onto the tiny alcove balcony like some lovesick teenager and pine for him. Or maybe the man was just flirting. Who knew?

"Mr. Love and his crew were up at dawn," Lacey said as she watched Lorna's face. "Surprising, since you and he went for such a long walk last night." Lifting a slanted brow, she added, "And...he must have really made an impression. You forgot your flashlight."

"The moon was full," Lorna retorted, not ready to explore her feelings for Mick with her overbearing sister. "I stayed close to Mick and everything was fine."

"Really?" Lacey looked doubtful. And concerned.

"Really," Lorna replied. "It's silly and hard to explain, but I felt...safe with Mick."

"That's not silly," Lacey said, her words soft with wonder, her eyes going tender. "That's amazing."

"Don't go reading anything into it." Lorna decided to change the subject. Nodding as one of the workers tipped his hard hat to them, she said, "They've certainly been working to get this place cleaned up."

Lacey took the hint, then bobbed her head. "See, they've managed to get the worst of the trees cleared away. And you'll be happy to know that most of the broken limbs will be recycled into mulch or, possibly used for firewood next winter. Nothing is going to waste around here."

Amid the noise of saws, grinders and shouting men, Lorna asked, "And what about the gardens? Has Lucas had a chance to talk to Justin yet?"

Justin Hayes was a very capable landscaper, if not a bit too possessive about the gardens. He watched everything from tender plants to the oldest trees with an eagle's eye. And he especially liked to keep an eye on Lacey. Which her stuck-up sister tended to ignore.

Justin wouldn't like having someone else messing with his landscaping. But Lucas knew how to handle Justin. They'd been fast friends since fourth grade.

"He's supposed to be talking with Justin right now, deciding what can be salvaged and what has to be pulled out," Lacey said.

Before they could continue the conversation, Mick

walked around the white, octagon-shaped summerhouse in the back garden near the restaurant's entrance. "Morning, ladies."

Lacey sent Lorna a quizzical look, then turned to greet Mick. "Hello, Mr. Love. Did you and your men get breakfast yet?"

"Yes, ma'am," Mick said, his eyes coming to rest on Lorna's face. "Rosie Lee passed out biscuits and ham and lots of that strong coffee you folks seem to like."

"We can make it less strong—that is, if you can't handle it," Lorna said, a teasing smile creasing her face.

She felt much better seeing Mick in the light of day. It proved that he was just a man, after all, and not some sort of mystic hero she'd dreamed up in the dark last night, come to protect her.

"I like it strong," Mick replied, his blue eyes focusing on her again. "How's the restaurant coming along?"

"It's slow going," Lorna told him. "In fact, my sister just came to get me away—seems I'm putting my nose into the repairs and harassing the workers, so she's forcing me to go help the needy. To bring out my docile side, I imagine."

"Does she have a docile side?" Mick asked Lacey.

His smile made Lorna think of mystic heroes all over again. He looked utterly charming, standing there in his work clothes, with his hard hat riding low over his wavy hair and sawdust covering him from head to toe. He might be mystic, but he was also very modern, and very much a real man. And he was teasing her, flirting with her again.

"It comes out every now and then," Lacey explained, giving her sister's arm a playful tug. "Our Lorna needs to relax and let all the relief workers do their work. I hope she hasn't been in your face already this morning."

"No," Mick replied, still looking at Lorna while he took the time to remove his hat and shake some of the dirt and dust off it. "In fact, I missed her at breakfast."

"I'm standing right here," Lorna said through a growl of frustration. "Y'all don't have to talk about me as if I'm not around. Feel free to include me in on the conversation regarding my lack of tact and manners."

"Has she had her coffee?" Mick asked Lacey, pointedly ignoring Lorna.

"I think she needs a little bit more," Lacey replied, deliberately talking over her sister's head.

Lorna was about to burst into a tirade, when Mick turned to her. "I'll buy you a cup."

"I have to go with my sister," she replied too sweetly.

He glanced back over his shoulder. "How about I drive into town with y'all. I can leave Josh in charge here. I've been wanting to survey the damage there, anyway. I might be able to lend a hand myself.''

"How thoughtful of you," Lacey said, nodding.

"Yes, how very thoughtful," Lorna echoed, sarcasm dripping from every word.

"I'm going to make sure Rosie Lee has the food ready, then I'll bring the truck around to get Aunt Hilda," Lacey told them. "Give me about twenty minutes."

"We'll be ready," Lorna said, wishing her sister would quit giving her those meaningful looks.

"You don't mind me tagging along, do you?" Mick asked Lorna when they were alone.

"Of course I don't mind."

She whirled to stalk into the summerhouse. The big rounded building boasted white wicker furniture with floral cushions and sheer white curtains that flapped in the breeze when all the French doors were thrown open. Lush tropical plants made the room look like part of the outdoors, which was why the summerhouse was such a popular extension of the restaurant. Several of the regular patrons often requested to dine at one of the more private bistro tables here.

Right now, Lorna only wanted to get the building back in shape, and put thoughts of Mick Love right out of her mind. But where to start?

Several hibiscus trees, some with bright pink flowers and others with rich reds, sat in clay pots all around the airy building. In one corner, a vivid orange bird-of-paradise plant hung over a white wicker breakfast table, while a moon vine—its white fragrant flowers now closed in a sleeping trumpet shape while they waited for darkness—clung to one of the intricately carved posts near the entrance way.

Lorna began picking up crushed hibiscus flowers. Someone had set the overturned pots back in their proper places and the muddy curtains had already been washed, bleached and hung back up, but the whole room still needed a good cleaning.

Mick's work boots clicked on the worn wooden floor.

"If you *don't* mind me being around, why are you in here attacking these poor plants?"

"I'm looking for dead-heads," Lorna explained, intent on doing something to stay busy. "The summerhouse is a favorite spot for our guests, and as you can clearly see, the wind blew one big mess of pine straw and magnolia leaves in here. I'm just surprised the storm didn't lift the whole thing up and destroy it, too."

She went about her work as she explained this, picking dead blossoms off the hibiscus trees, bending to pick up wilted flowers, then tossing it all out when her hands got too full.

"Tornadoes are like that," Mick said as he put his hard hat down and stooped to help her. "All fury in one place, then hardly lifting a twig in another."

Lorna kept right on cleaning. She found the big

push-broom one of Rosie Lee's daughter's had left out here yesterday and started moving it across the polished hardwood floor. The others had already taken the braided rugs up to wash and dry, too. The entire building had been filled with mud and dirt, the wind having blown right through the open doors and windows.

When she reached the main entrance door, she found Mick standing there blocking her way.

"Yep, tornadoes are a lot like women."

That remark, made with a smirk, brought her head up. "Are you comparing me to that storm that ripped through here?"

"Maybe."

"And why would you do that?"

"Maybe because you seemed like a whirlwind this morning yourself. Was it something I said?"

Lorna stood there holding the broom, her heart pumping as if she were indeed about to take off in a mad wind. "Actually, it's several things you've said, and it's the way you've been acting."

"Oh, and how's that?"

"You...you're deliberately flirting with me, teasing me. It's your fault if I'm acting like a cyclone. I don't understand what you're trying to prove."

"So...do you always go into a flying tizzy every time a man comes near you?"

She wanted to send the broom flying at him. Honestly, Lorna didn't know why she felt so scattered, so angry. Maybe because she liked order, and there didn't seem to be any here right now. "No, I do not. It's just that—"

He stepped closer, his hand coming down over hers to hold the broom handle between them. "It's just that you feel it, too, right?"

"Feel…what?"

"Us," he replied, his blue eyes the color of the bearded irises growing down near the swamp basin.

"Us?" She repeated the little word, understanding with a fast-beating heart its big meaning. "There is no 'us,' Mick."

"I think there might be, if you'll just relax a little bit."

"You can't be serious," she said, a tiny hint of breath escaping as she tried to find air.

But breathing was near impossible, with him standing there so close. She could see the sawdust in his hair, see the flecks of triumph in his eyes.

"I'm very serious," Mick replied, reaching up to pull a long strand of hair away from her flushed face.

"We've know each other—what, twenty-four hours?" Lorna asked, trying to sound logical. But it came out more like an awe-filled statement than a logical question.

"That's the strangest thing," Mick replied, his fingers moving through her hair as he placed the lost locks back on her shoulder. "It's weird, what with you telling me off all the time, but I just like being around you, Lorna.''

''That's preposterous.''

''You said you were praying. You said God sent me to you. What did you mean by that?''

She tried to move away, but his hand held her there. ''I meant…I meant that we needed help, and God sent someone who could help us.''

''But it's more than that, don't you think?''

Oh, she not only thought it. She knew it in her heart. She'd walked in the moonlight with this man, then gone inside only to feel empty and alone. She'd asked God to help her find her center again, to calm her fears as He'd always done. She'd asked God to let her see His reasoning for bringing Mick Love here. She wanted to understand why this man made her pulse weak and her heart race.

Had God sent Mick to her?

The way Mick stood looking at her now, she wanted to believe that. But then, she'd made so many mistakes before, with so many men. She'd always fallen in love much too quickly, only to realize too late that it wasn't right. So she panicked and pushed them away. Lorna never let things get out of control, out of hand, except in the love department—there she rushed headlong into disaster, only to bring things to a skidding halt before anyone could get too close.

But after Paris, after Cole had broken off their wedding, she'd been very careful around men. Or, at least, she had been up until now. Now, she had to keep things in perspective.

For the past few years, she'd been tucked away here, safe and content. She'd put any thoughts of love out of her mind, since her last relationship had ended on a very bitter note. Since then, she'd learned to stay in control.

But with Mick, she couldn't seem to find any control. And with Mick, things seemed different. Whereas before, she dated men to prove that she was capable of being intimate, of having a relationship, now she wasn't so sure about any of that. Now, she really didn't want her heart to talk her into anything she'd regret. Maybe that was the difference. Her heart was doing the talking now. Before, she'd always been impulsive, jumping into a relationship simply because she thought she *needed* to be in one. She had always thought being with a man was just the next logical step, but being involved had never seemed to work out logically. She'd learned that the hard way.

"I said, what do you think?" Mick asked again, bringing her out of her rambling thoughts.

"I think you are...*impossible*." She stressed the French pronunciation of the word.

"Don't go using that foreign language on me."

"Well, since you don't seem to understand English—"

He tugged her close, his hands pulling through her loosely braided hair. "I understand that I like being with you. I understand that you seem to like being with me. But other than that, there's a whole lot I don't understand. But I'm willing to stick around to find out the rest.''

''Don't waste your time,'' Lorna told him. ''I usually send men running in the other direction.''

''I can't imagine why.''

''See, there you go teasing me again.'' She managed to pull away this time, her broom intact. ''Maybe I should explain how things work with me, Mick. I've been engaged…oh, let's see…three times. I called off two of them, and the last one jilted me at the altar. And in between, I've dated for a few weeks, maybe months, but then suddenly, each time, I decided I was tired of the relationship and sent my suitor packing. For some reason, in spite of my earnest prayers for God to send me someone to spend the rest of my life with, I can't seem to make the right connection.''

''Well, maybe you've been praying for the wrong things.''

That comment astounded her. ''And what would *you* know about prayer?''

She regretted asking the question, especially when she saw the hurt and anger warring in his eyes.

''More than you might think,'' he told her. Then he leaned back against the door frame and crossed his arms over his chest. ''I used to pray, every night in that matchbox trailer my mother and I called a home.

I used to ask God to explain to me why my old man had turned out to be such a louse and why my mother had to suffer every day of her life. But I never got any answers to those prayers. So I quit asking and I quit depending on God to help me out. I struggled and I worked and I finally made something of myself—"

He stopped, took a deep breath, then threw up his hands. "Look, just forget it, all right. It sounds like you've been burned just as badly as I have, and I sure don't need to be reminded of that. Or the fact that we don't have a whole lot in common. We're not the same, you and me. Not from the same stock." He shrugged, grabbed up his hat. "I was just flirting. Just killing time with a pretty woman. I won't bother you again."

And with that, he was gone.

Lorna stood there, flabbergasted, clinging to her broom, while the gentle morning breeze lifted the white lace sheers of the summerhouse and sent them trailing after him like a bride's veil tossed in the wind.

Chapter Six

Before Lorna could go after Mick to tell him she was sorry, Lacey came rushing down the winding garden path toward the summerhouse, her floral skirt lifting all around her slender calves as she ran.

"We have to go, Lorna. There's been some trouble in town. Several people were cleaning up some of the debris and...a building caved in. They think someone is trapped inside."

"Oh, no." Lorna dropped her broom, then hurried toward Lacey. "Where's Aunt Hilda?"

"In the truck," Lacey told her, tugging her up the path.

They met Josh Simmons on the way to the car. "Ladies," he said, tipping his hard hat, a wide smile on his dark face. Then he noticed their concerned expressions. "Something wrong?"

"Accident in town," Lacey said over her shoulder. "We have to hurry."

"I'll come, too," Josh told them. "Want me to get Mick?"

"We could use the help," Lorna called, hoping Josh would be able to find Mick. After their confrontation, she wasn't sure he'd stick around Bayou le Jardin much longer. Why had she said such hateful things to him, anyway?

Why, indeed? Didn't she always manage to send men running with a few choice words? Mick probably wouldn't be any different from the rest. Apparently, he'd suffered through some bad spots himself. Wondering about his comments—living in a trailer park, his father's wrath and…being of different stock— only made her want to get to know him better, to show him that she wasn't a blue-blooded snob. But Lorna knew she could never really explain herself to Mick. That would mean having to tell him about her many flaws, and that usually did the trick for her in the love department. Maybe it was for the best that he'd seen her callous side so soon. That way, they wouldn't start something they could never finish.

"I thought Mick was with you," Lacey said as she ran toward the utility vehicle they used to get around the vast property.

Lorna headed for the front passenger seat, knowing Aunt Hilda preferred the back seat. "He…he had things to do. I'm sure he and Josh will follow us."

As they both hopped into the truck, they heard Aunt Hilda talking on her cell phone. "What do you mean? Why was Kathryn there? Oh, my. Oh, my. We're on our way."

"What's wrong?" Lacey asked, glancing in the rearview mirror as she cranked the big vehicle around, then took off down the winding gravel drive toward the old River Road.

"The building… They think Kathryn might be the one trapped inside." Aunt Hilda held a wrinkled hand to her heart. "She was helping a child look for her kitten."

"Kathryn?" Lorna glanced over at Lacey. Her sister shot her a worried, pale look that only mirrored the sick feeling in the pit of her own stomach. "Do they know for sure?"

"No," Aunt Hilda replied, shaking her head. "They only know she was headed in that direction…and then a few minutes later they heard a crash and the wall caved in. Oh, I've told Kathryn to be careful, to stay away from the clean-up efforts. Why didn't she listen to me?"

"Because she's a hard worker, and she loves animals," Lorna replied, turning to give her aunt a pat on the arm. "We'll find her, Aunt Hilda. Try to stay calm."

"I'm perfectly calm," her aunt told her. "But you both know how I feel about Kathryn."

Yes, Lorna knew how much her aunt loved her

young assistant. Hilda Dorsette had been a mentor to Kathryn Sonnier since Kathryn's days in middle school. Kathryn was a beautiful African-American child who'd come from a poor family. Her mother had wanted Kathryn to have a better life than the one she'd had, so she had encouraged her daughter to do well in school. When Kathryn's teacher sent out a call for mentors to help some of her struggling students, Aunt Hilda had signed up right away. And since that day more than thirteen years ago, Aunt Hilda had seen Kathryn through high school and college, funding most of her endeavors in a quiet, behind-the-scenes way. And she had promised Kathryn a job when she finished college.

Kathryn had worked her way up from front-desk clerk to assistant to the mayor in just under three years. Aunt Hilda loved the young woman just as much as she loved all the Dorsettes and the Babineaux. And Kathryn felt the same way about Hilda. She was a good assistant, and the protector at the gate when it came to people harassing the small town's lovable mayor.

If anything happened to Kathryn...

"I hope she's okay," Lacey said, as if reading Lorna's mind.

Soon, they neared the small community that was located just around the bend from the bed-and-breakfast.

"It's the general store," Aunt Hilda said, craning

her neck to see. "It got hit pretty bad—they had to condemn it. I don't know if Jesse will be able to rebuild or not, and now this."

"She can't take much more," Lorna said underneath her breath to Lacey, as they pulled up to where a crowd was gathered in front of the damaged building.

Lorna hated seeing the distress in her aunt's sweet eyes. Aunt Hilda was their rock—she held them all together, just as Mick had suggested. Lorna had taken that for granted over the years, but since she'd come back home she'd learned to appreciate her aunt. Now, Lorna felt the fingers of her unnamed fears surrounding her again. What would they do if they lost Aunt Hilda?

Asking God to put that particular scenario out of her mind, Lorna instead concentrated on the matter at hand. They had to find out if Kathryn was in that building. And if she was, they had to save her.

Mick pulled up his Chevy pickup underneath a towering oak tree near what was left of the quaint little town square in Jardin. A road sign hung next to an historical marker citing the population as 1,003. Mick was only interested in finding one of those 1,000 or so people. Turning off the roaring motor of the truck, he scanned the crowd gathered at the dilapidated remains of what used to be Jesse's General Store of Jardin.

"Let's see if we can find Lorna and Lacey," he told Josh, as they hopped out of the big-wheeled truck, hard hats in their hands. They'd left the rest of the crew back at the mansion to clear away the broken limbs near Lorna's bedroom so the contractor could get to the roof and make necessary repairs.

"Yeah," Josh replied, squinting toward the morning sun. "They were pretty shook up when I saw them."

"I guess so," Mick replied. At least, he imagined Lorna was still shaken from their earlier conversation, and he was sure hearing about this accident hadn't helped matters.

And now that he'd blurted out the details of his measly life, he was also sure Lorna Dorsette would no longer have anything to do with him. He wasn't good enough for the likes of her. She was a lady, pure and simple, first-class all the way, while he was a first-class fool for even entertaining the notion of getting to know her.

And yet, he searched for her long red hair in the crowd. He wanted to help her. "There they are," he told Josh, grabbing his friend by the sleeve to urge him forward.

Lorna looked up. She was standing near the cave-in where several men were trying to dig through the rubble. "Mick," she called, waving a hand for him and Josh.

Mick hurried over, nodding his head to Lacey and

Aunt Hilda. "How bad is it?" he asked in a low voice.

"Pretty bad," Lorna told him, her green eyes bright with fear and worry. "My aunt's assistant, Kathryn Sonnier, is down there. She went in after a kitten. They were bulldozing some debris close by, and the movement must have made the wall shift. She's alive—we've talked to her, but they can't seem to get to her, and she's been awfully quiet the past few minutes." She motioned toward the men. "We only have a volunteer fire department—they're all loyal and well-trained, but we've never had anything such as this. The National Guard hasn't arrived here yet, so all we can do is wait for the ambulance to come from Kenner."

Mick put a hand on Lorna's shoulder. "What can we do?"

One of the men, a robust fellow with a bulging belly, stood up and turned to Mick. Out of breath from trying to remove broken bricks and timbers, he said, "Well, son, you and your friend there are a might bit skinnier than the rest of us. We need someone to squeeze in there and help Kathryn up. We can get her out through this path we've cleared, but she thinks she broke her leg, and she can't find the strength to move. The whole thing isn't very stable, though. If we don't hurry, she might get buried in there."

"I'll go in," Josh said as he marched up to the

other man. "I worked as a volunteer fireman a few years ago—before Mick gave me a job."

"Are you sure?" Lorna asked Josh.

Mick pushed his friend forward, hoping to lighten the concern in her eyes. "Look at him. Tall and lanky, and he can shimmy like a snake. We used to hide in the kudzu vines near the railroad tracks, and Josh always found the best hiding places."

Josh grinned. "And speaking of snakes, I saw a few. But listen, we can talk about all of that later. Tell me what to do."

The big fellow, named Ralph, proceeded to explain. "We were tearing away the damaged walls from the video store when we heard the crash. We came right over and called out. That's when we found out from a little girl standing nearby that Kathryn was down there. But we can't seem to get in to see how badly she's hurt. We're just lucky the kid didn't go down in there with her."

He motioned to the doctor, a feeble old man with a tuft of white hair combed at an exaggerated sideways slant across his ruddy brow. "And Doc Howard ain't able to climb down in that mess." Then he turned back to Josh. "If you can get in, then move the debris that's got her trapped or at least pull her out from it, we can send a rope and stretcher down to make a pulley so we can lift her up."

"And I can give you instructions on how to splint

her leg so she won't damage it further,'' Dr. Howard told Josh.

"Okay," Josh said, already stepping into the shadowy opening. "I've set a broken arm before. A leg can't be much different."

He got halfway down the hole, then called, "Kathryn, can you hear me? My name is Josh, and I'm coming in after you."

"Yes" came the weak reply. "Are you going to get me out of here?"

"I'm going to try," Josh told her, holding a hand to his hard hat. "Just stay calm, honey. This might take a while, but I'm coming down there so I can get some of that mess off you and see how badly you're hurt."

"Okay." Then on a feeble plea, she added, "Please hurry."

Mick watched as his friend started pushing debris out of the way. "Josh, be careful."

Josh gave him the thumbs-up. "Hey, buddy, we been in tighter spots, don't you know?"

"I do know," Mick replied, trying to muster up a smile of his own. "Bring her out—and hey, don't flirt with her too much."

"Right," Josh said, just before he disappeared from sight down the V-shaped passageway between the collapsed wall and the remains of the building's foundation.

Mick looked up from the narrow opening to find

Lorna's eyes on him. He thought he saw gratitude there, and maybe a little understanding. Then again, maybe it was just his imagination working overtime.

"Thank you for coming," she said, her whisper for his ears only. "Kathryn is a very special person. My aunt would be devastated if anything happened to her."

"Josh will bring her out," Mick told her, as they waited. "And I'm right here if they need me."

"You always seem to be in the right place at the right time."

"Or the wrong place at the wrong time, depending on how you look at things."

"I don't always see things so clearly," she replied. Then she turned away, her eyes moving over the collapsed building in front of them.

Was that her way of apologizing for her earlier harsh words? Well, she'd been right. He certainly wasn't an authority on religion and prayer. And he hadn't depended on God's help or strength for a very long time.

And Lorna seemed to thrive on those very things.

He wanted to ask her if she really did understand. Make her see that although he'd lagged behind in the faith department, he wasn't a bad person.

Mick didn't question her, though. Now wasn't the time. Instead, he just reached out and took her hand.

After a few minutes, he called to Josh. "Hey, man, what's going on down there? You're way too quiet."

He got a grunt in reply. "Tight space…can't talk right now."

Mick pulled Lorna with him so they could peer down the narrow opening. "It looks like the wall fell in right over some steps."

"The storage room," Lorna told him. "Jesse had a basement down below." Then she explained that Kathryn had probably been moving down the narrow basement stairs when the wall just to the left had given way. "They think a bulldozer moving rubble from the video store shook the wall and triggered the collapse, just as Kathryn leaned down the steps to look for the kitten." She shrugged, her green eyes like a dark, mysterious forest. "We found the kitten right away." She pointed to where a little dark-haired girl held tightly to the meowing cat. "And thankfully, Kathryn made the child stay far away from the building."

Mick nodded, then glanced around. "Where's that ambulance?"

"They're on their way," Lorna told him. "They have to come from Kenner, about fifteen miles away."

"Are any of your volunteers trained for a medical emergency?"

"They're all trained, but only one is in the best of shape to handle something like this—and he had to go out of town before the storm hit. He's been trying to get back, but…" She stopped, looked toward where Aunt Hilda was sitting on a chair in the shade with Lacey watching over her. "Our aunt is trying to obtain funds for a new fire station. We managed to get a two-man police department a few years back, but it's tough to get much else out here, so we have to rely on volunteers. They're pretty dependable, but they've never had to deal with something like this."

Mick nodded. "And they don't look as fit as big city firemen."

"No," Lorna replied. "They work hard and mean well, but we really need someone to come in and take charge, get them up to standard."

The small talk kept Mick sane, while the grunts and distant words of his friend drifted up to him now and again. Jesse, the owner of the store, and Doc Howard both kept calling out to make sure Josh was okay.

After what seemed like hours, they heard Josh's excited shout. "I've found her. Send down the rope and pulley. Might need a scoop stretcher—this space is tight—and the equipment to make a splint. Her leg is definitely broken."

The doctor and several other people went to work gathering the needed supplies and securing them onto a board that Mick helped to send down the narrow passage to his friend.

"Here it comes," Mick shouted to Josh. "Can you reach it?"

They heard a shuffling noise, then Josh called out, "Got it."

Mick breathed a sigh of relief, then wiped the dust from his perspiring face. "That Josh, always rushing in. He did that when we were growing up, too."

"You two grew up together?"

He glanced over at Lorna, ready to see scorn or condemnation on her face. Instead, he saw a questioning look, as if she really were interested in knowing. And she *should* know: She should see right away that Mick Love wasn't her type at all.

Even if Mick Love suddenly wanted to be the man of her dreams.

Knowing how upset she was, he decided to keep her distracted with mundane chitchat. That would help calm his own knife-edged worry, too, he guessed. He hoped. "Yeah, we lived in the same trailer park, near the Pearl River. Floods used to get us just about every spring."

"We've had a few flood scares ourselves, living on the Mississippi," she told him.

Mick tried to compare living at Bayou le Jardin with living in a run-down trailer park. Flood or not, there was no comparison. He put that particular issue aside for now and continued the conversation on a low, even tone.

"Josh and I did everything together," he said, a flash of memory making him shake his head. "Went to school together, then skipped school together. Got into all kinds of trouble. Until our mommas pooled their resources and put us in church each Sunday."

He saw the surprise in her eyes, coupled with regret.

"It seems I misjudged you...before."

"No, you pretty much nailed me," he replied, unsmiling. "I haven't been very devout in my faith as an adult. Now, being a child was a different thing. My momma saw to it that I understood right from wrong."

He grinned and was rewarded with one of her dazzling smiles.

"And did you see the error of your ways?" she asked quietly and without judgment.

"Pretty much, but we kept getting into trouble. Josh comes from a big family, and I used to hang out at his house. His momma can sure cook."

"Didn't seem to stick with him," she replied, nodding toward the hole Josh had disappeared down. "He's in good shape."

"He's very athletic."

"I guess you'd both have to be, what with the business you're in."

"Yep."

In spite of the easy banter, Mick could see the worry coloring Lorna's brilliant eyes a deeper shade of green. "They'll make it," he told her, pulling her close. "Josh knows what he's doing."

"I hope so," she said, turning to give her sister a

quick smile. "My aunt isn't taking this very well. She's held up so wonderfully through all of this, but—"

Just then they heard a shout from Josh. And then a loud rumble moved through the broken building. Lorna rushed forward, but Mick held her back as the timbers and bricks around them seemed to shudder and sway, dirt and dust lifting up in a choking cloud that temporarily blinded them. Then a deadly silence fell over the shrouded mass of wood and stone.

"Kathryn?" Lorna shouted. When she didn't get an answer she leaned forward, closer. "Kathryn, say something!"

Mick stepped up, still holding her. "Josh, buddy, you'd better talk to me!"

Nothing.

Behind them now, Lacey stood holding Aunt Hilda's hand, waiting with a look of dread on her face as she tried to keep her aunt still and calm.

"We have to do something," Lorna said, clutching Mick, terror underscoring each word.

Mick acted on instinct and adrenaline. Pushing Lorna into the arms of the surprised doctor, he shoved on his hard hat, then pressed his lower body into the tight opening, calling to his friend as he went. "Josh, are you all right? Joshua Clarence Simmons, you'd better answer me. Right now, and I mean it."

Mick couldn't explain the sick feeling of dread, didn't stop to think about it. It moved like an electrical jolt through his entire system as he entered that dark, dusty hole. But he had to find Josh and Kathryn. Alive. He didn't even realize he'd started praying. But the words were forming in his head as quickly as the dust had formed on his body.

"Dear God, help them. Help me."

"Mick, don't go in there!"

Lorna's voice was the last thing he heard as he descended into the pitch-black alleyway of twisted metal and broken glass and boards, determined to find his friend and Kathryn.

And even more determined to get back to Lorna Dorsette once this was all over.

Chapter Seven

He remembered a face. A face with long red-blond hair, and eyes the color of a summer meadow—green and lush, rich with hope and promise. He could hear her voice calling to him. Or was he just having a wonderful, peaceful dream.

"Mick, can you hear me? It's Lorna."

Mick opened his burning, heavy-lidded eyes to find Lorna bent over him, her long hair falling in gentle curls and waves around her face and shoulders, her perfume reminding him of magnolias and honeysuckle...a garden.

Bayou le Jardin.

Then the memories came swirling by like a black fog. He bolted upright, but his head hurt so badly, he couldn't see straight. Reaching up, he found a bloody knot the size of a hen's egg just above his right temple.

Lorna's arms on his brought him back down. "Take it easy, Mick."

"Where am I?"

"On a couch in Aunt Hilda's office at City Hall. You lost your hat and hit your head. Doc thinks you have a mild concussion. We really should get you to the emergency room."

"Where's...?" He couldn't form the words, so he just looked up at her, sure he'd see the answers he needed in her gentle face, but not sure he wanted to know them.

Then, because he was afraid of the news, Mick glanced out the door of the tiny office to a small reception area with two large ficus trees on each side of the glass doors. A sign on the wall gave directions to the mayor's office and the business office. Everything looked so normal. He could hear voices in another part of the building, a phone ringing off in the distance.

Then he looked back at Lorna. "Are they all right?"

"Josh and Kathryn are safe. They took them to the emergency room in Kenner. Mick, you saved their lives."

His throat felt as rough and dry as tree bark. But welcome relief flowed over him, causing him to relax back against the floral cushions someone had placed beneath his head. "Oh, yeah, and how'd I do that?"

Lorna sat down next to him on the wide vinyl couch, so near that a thick mass of her hair brushed Mick's forearm, making him think of angel's wings and harp strings.

"We're really not sure," she said, her own voice shaky and strained. "One minute you were there, the next you were gone down that hole. We heard you shouting for Josh, then you called out to us that you'd found them. Josh was unconscious, but somehow, you got him out of the way, moved a timber beam off Kathryn, then lifted her, maybe dragged her to safety."

"But...her leg?"

"You didn't have time to worry about that. The building was very unstable. Her leg is broken, and she's got bruises and cuts, but she's going to be okay."

"And Josh?"

"He's all right, too. He'd just found Kathryn and was trying to set her leg, when the building gave way again. His hard hat saved him from having a concussion, too, according to Doc. But he threw his body over Kathryn's, so he's got a long gash on one arm and some cuts across his shoulder. They were concerned about him losing so much blood."

Mick looked down at his own shirt. It was stained a dark red. The memory of touching his friend, only to find him covered in blood, made him queasy. But he tried to sit up again. "I have to go see about him."

"Whoa." Lorna pushed him back down with surprising force for someone so petite and small framed. "It's bad enough that you insisted the ambulance take them first, but you still need to be checked over."

She shook her head, obviously amazed at what he'd done. "You kept telling us you were all right, so we sent the ambulance away. Then you passed out on us when we were trying to check your head. So just stay put." She waited for him to settle down, then explained, "The only reason you aren't headed to the hospital yourself is that Doc assured me you'd be all right. But I have very strict orders to keep a close eye on you." She stayed right beside him, as if daring him to move. "As soon as you get your bearings, I'm driving you into Kenner to make sure Doc's diagnosis is correct."

"Good, then I can see Josh, make sure he's okay."

"That's fair enough," she replied, nodding. Then a worried look creased her brow. "Are you sure you're really all right? I mean, how do you feel right now?"

Mick couldn't begin to answer that question. She was too near, and he was still too shaky. But right now, this very minute, he felt as if a voice had indeed come to him and whispered in his ear. *"It's not your time, Mick. You have to do this. You have to save them and yourself."*

Had he imagined that, there in the dark bowels of that ravaged building? How had he managed to get Josh out of the way in spite of all the blood, remove that heavy timber beam, then get Kathryn hoisted onto the stretcher? He didn't even remember dragging her onto it there in the semidarkness and dust. How had he managed to do that, then get her up to safety?

"It's all so foggy," he said now. "I don't know what happened, really. I just remember thinking I had to hurry."

"You called out to us," Lorna said. She sat back, her arms wrapped around her midsection, her eyes wide with memories and anxiety. "Jesse and Ralph pulled on the stretcher rope, then Lucas showed up and helped them tug Kathryn up. She was lying across the board on her stomach, but you'd managed to get her broken leg up on the board so it didn't drag. Doc said that helped, but the pain caused her to pass out."

Pain. He did remember a burst of pain. "How did I hit my head?"

"I don't know," she replied, still clutching herself, staring down at a spot on the patterned carpet. "Probably some falling debris when you started climbing out. We kept hearing rumbles, things falling."

Then she looked back up and right into his eyes. "You scared me, Mick. I thought…"

"Shh," he said, taking her arms to pull her hands away from her body. Her fingers felt both icy and clammy. "It's over now. We're all safe. It's going to be okay."

"Thanks to you. This is the second time you've come to the rescue for us. I won't forget it."

His head was swimming again, but not from the concussion. This dizziness came from the look in Lorna's eyes, that vulnerable look of a lost child, that confused and dazed look of someone searching for answers in the dark. That look that shattered him and battered him and made him want to pull her into his arms and hold her tightly.

Right now, their differences didn't matter. Right now, although he knew it was wrong, he didn't want to walk away from what he was feeling. He wasn't nearly good enough for her, would never measure up. And yet, he was willing to try.

He knew it would be tough. She'd told him about her other relationships. Engagements that had failed. And apparently, one trip to the altar that had turned out badly. She was trying to forget all of that, and in doing so, she was denying everything between them.

He didn't want her to forget. He didn't want her to deny. He didn't want her to forget *him* or deny *him.* Because he'd surely never forget her. And he could no longer deny his own erratic feelings.

And after being down in that dark, tight space with little air and little confidence, with his life flashing in slow-motion before him and his best friend bleeding and hurt, he knew that he had to have her by his side—somehow.

So he let go of her hand, then reached up a finger to touch her cheek. "Hey, you know something?"

Her eyes widened. "What?"

"When I went down there, I wasn't thinking about anything in particular—I just had to help Josh and Kathryn."

She nodded, her gaze searching.

"But I do remember this—I remember thinking that if I ever got out of there alive, I'd do something I've been wanting to do since the first time I held you in my arms."

Her eyelashes fluttered against her cheeks. Letting her gaze drop, she refused to look at him. "Oh, and what's that?"

"This—" he said, as he lifted her head with his thumb. Then with his other hand, he pulled her head down. "This—" he repeated, the one word caught on a low, husky growl. Then he kissed her, his mouth lifting, then returning to hers until he'd settled his lips against hers in a gesture of pure pleasure and deep-seeded longing.

He was dizzy again, reeling in a sweet-smelling, soft-to-the-touch dream. A dream filled with moonlight and flowers and a river flowing nearby. A dream of her taking his hand in the dark and holding him forever.

Lorna sighed against him, kissed him back with the

same softness and tenderness he'd seen in her eyes that first day. But he could feel the tentative fear he'd also seen like a dark aura surrounding her.

He wanted to capture that fear and turn it into something else. He wanted to change that fear to a steadfast joy. If he could kiss it away, he would. But he had a distinct feeling that it would take more than kisses to win this woman's heart.

So he stopped kissing her, then pulled her close and held her near his own erratic heart.

She sank against him, then sighed, content for now it seemed.

Or so he thought. She turned her head, her breath brushing on his ear like spring flowers moving in the wind, while her angry words rolled over him like a tide changing. "Don't ever do that to me again, Mick Love."

Lorna got up, seeking air, breath, control. This couldn't be happening. It was too fast, much too fast. Faster, quicker than any of her other so-called relationships. Her heart was beating too fast, her breath was coming too fast. And the kiss—oh, that had happened way too fast. And ended much too soon. But this had to end. Now.

Mick held her arm, wouldn't let go. "Are you going to deny this? That you've wanted the same thing since the day we met? Are you going to tell me you didn't enjoy that kiss just as much as I did?"

Lorna took one hand and daintily removed Mick's tanned, veined hand from her wrist. Then she lapsed into French. *"Cochon! Imbecile!"*

"Hey, it was just a kiss. No need for name-calling."

She turned then to see the hurt Mick quickly tried to erase. *"Stupide*—don't be stupid. I'm not talking about the kiss, and I'm not calling you names—those are aimed at me for being so foolish. What I was trying to say—" She threw up her hands, ran them over her hair. "Don't ever scare me like that again. When you went into that building, my heart stopped."

The lopsided grin on his face made her heart stop all over again.

"Oh, that. It was nothing, really. Let's get back to the important stuff. So, you did enjoy the kiss?"

"Now, you find this amusing—*now,* after I was so helpless and horrified. Oh, you're impossible!"

"I think you've told me that before."

Gaining strength with distance, she said, "That's because it's true. You went down there, risking your life—"

"I had to help Josh."

"I understand," she said, trying to find the words that would describe all the emotions she'd been through in the past couple of hours. "I can't explain it," she said, throwing her hands up again. "I can't explain this—" she pointed to her lips, still swollen and tingling from their kiss "—I can't explain this—'' she held her hand to her heart. Then she sank down on a nearby chair. "I feel as if I'm the one with a bump on the head—and stop grinning at me!"

"I can't help it," he told her, still grinning. "You are so beautiful. Especially when you've just been kissed."

She got up to come and stand over him, wagging a finger in his face. "Well, don't go getting any crazy ideas."

Mick grabbed her hand, urged her down onto the couch beside him. "Oh, I've got several ideas—some crazy, some completely sane."

Lorna inhaled deeply, bracing herself for another onslaught of gale-force kisses. "Put them out of your mind. I'm taking you to the hospital."

He let her go. "Yep, maybe I do need my head examined, at that."

She didn't miss the trace of sarcasm in his words. Did he already regret kissing her? Did she really, truly care?

She realized she did. And that put the tremendous, unnamed fear back in her heart, quickly replacing the wonderful sensations that being in his arms had awakened.

Wanting to get back to business and back in control of her senses, she said, "Lucas took Lacey and Aunt Hilda to the medical center in Kenner to be with Kathryn. Can you manage to walk to the front door and wait, while I pull the truck around?"

"I think I can manage that, thank you," he said, raising himself up off the couch. The effort caused his dark skin to turn pale, however. "Whew, I'm hurting in places I didn't even know I had, but at least the room isn't tilting and swaying anymore."

Not trusting him, Lorna took his arm. "You're obviously still in a lot of pain. You'll be sore and bruised for a while, no doubt." Then she softened her tone. "Here, lean on me."

Mick looked over at her, his blue eyes filled with an unreadable message—longing, a search, and finally, a resigned kind of quietness. But before she could prop him against a white column outside the front door of the small City Hall office, he grabbed her hand again. "This isn't over Lorna. Not by a long shot."

"It has to be over, Mick," she replied. "We both got a little carried away in there, that's all. Too much excitement."

"If that's what you want to believe," he replied, his eyes never wavering.

Lorna hurried to find the truck. *Lord, I don't know what's happening to me,* she silently prayed. *Help me. I'm so scared. I've never felt like this before. What does it mean?*

On her way to the truck, she glanced over at the remains of the general store. The building was completely ruined now, caved in on itself like a giant cracker box that had gotten caught in a trash compactor.

Mick had been inside that crushed mess.

He could have died.

He and Josh and Kathryn—they all could have died.

Her hands shaking, Lorna suddenly realized what the great fear clawing at her gut was really about.

She was falling in love with Mick Love.

She couldn't fall in love with Mick.

Because she couldn't bear to lose him.

Better to keep her distance, and keep things under control. Then she'd never have to suffer again—the way she'd suffered when her parents had been so brutally taken from her, the way she'd suffered during the raging storm, and the way she'd suffered this morning.

And that was it in a nutshell. That was why she'd always run away from a serious commitment. That was why she'd called off her so-called engagements. And ultimately, that was why she'd been left at the altar.

A blessing in disguise, no doubt.

If she refused to acknowledge how Mick made her feel, she'd never again have to stand over a pile of rubble and know that the man she was falling for could become buried deep inside, away from her touch, hurt and helpless in a small, dust-filled hole.

Long ago, Lorna had made a promise to herself that she'd never again be left alone in the dark.

If she fell for Mick, then lost him, that's exactly where she'd be—back in the dark. And she wouldn't go through that again. Ever.

Chapter Eight

"How can we ever repay you?"

Hilda Dorsette stood in the hospital lobby, her hand on Mick's arm, her eyes misty with gratitude. She was making him extremely nervous.

"You don't have to repay me, Miss Hilda. I just did what anyone would have done."

"You were very brave," Hilda replied, her wrinkled, bejeweled hand still clutching his. "How's your head?"

"Hard as a rock," Mick joked, embarrassed by all the fuss he'd received since he and Lorna had arrived at the bustling medical center in nearby Kenner.

The media had been there, asking a million redundant questions.

"*...Mr. Love, what went through your mind as you plunged down into that dark abyss?*"

"...Mr. Love, how did you manage to rescue two people without getting seriously hurt yourself?"

What did they expect him to say? What could he say? How could he explain? Now, Mick couldn't even remember what he'd told the excited reporters. It didn't matter, anyway.

He only wanted to find Lorna and go back to the peace and quiet of Bayou le Jardin. But it looked like that might not happen any time soon.

The family had all been here—all the Dorsettes and the Babineaux, even Kathryn's grateful mother Polly, cooing and aahing over him and embellishing his rescue efforts into a dramatic tale full of excitement and daring deeds—before they'd all scattered for lunch and visits with Kathryn.

Except for Lorna, of course. Since she'd brought him to the emergency room and been assured by several doctors that he wasn't seriously hurt, she'd managed to find all sorts of excuses for steering clear of Mick. Oh, she had to call to talk to the contractors about the restaurant repairs. She had to make sure her vendors wouldn't make deliveries until all was clear. She had to see that no guests were booked to stay at the mansion or in the cottages until the repairs and cleanup could be completed.... Mick had watched her, amused and disturbed, as she pushed buttons on her cell phone with all the buzzing energy of a honeybee, her gaze averted from his all the while.

Lorna was still stewing about that kiss, he reckoned. He'd known better than to kiss the woman, but he couldn't help himself. He'd needed that kiss as much as he'd needed his next breath. And he intended to kiss her again, lots. But that particular goal would have to wait until all this excitement and praise settled down.

Mick didn't want any praise. He just wanted to make sure Josh and Kathryn were safe and well. But now, Hilda Dorsette herself was thanking Mick and promising him a key to the city, so he had to be polite and give her his undivided attention. Hilda Dorsette commanded that kind of respect, and Mick certainly had enough manners to give it to her. She was worried about her town, so she appreciated his efforts.

"Can't you see?" she said now, her eyes watering. "What you did gave new hope to all those who lost so much in this storm. We found a tiny bit of triumph in the midst of our despair. And for that, I will be eternally grateful."

Touched, Mick could only smile and nod. "Really, now, Miss Hilda, don't make me out to be something I'm not. We had a lot of help. Josh was much braver than me."

"He'll be rewarded as well, believe me." She tugged Mick to a nearby floral divan. "Have you noticed how Josh refuses to leave Kathryn's side? I think those two made a match down there in that rubble."

Mick sat back on the comfortable couch, then lifted a brow. "A match? Buried underneath a building?"

"The Lord works His ways, even in the darkness, Mr. Love."

He couldn't argue with that logic. Since he'd come to Bayou le Jardin, Mick had felt the Lord's presence all around him, both night and day. And it was making him crazy. In a good way, of course. For the first time in his life, Mick was beginning to understand what it meant to have a loving, supportive family gathered around you. And he liked that notion a whole lot, even if it did scare him. Even if he knew in his heart that he could never be a part of this particular family.

He liked Lorna Dorsette a whole lot, too. And that definitely scared him. He'd be leaving soon, so how was he supposed to continue things? Did he dare to hope that he might have a chance?

"You looked a bit confused," Hilda said, her appraising stare never wavering. "Are you sure you're feeling better?"

Mick touched the bandaged place on his head. "It still hurts, but I'm fine, really. Just a bit overwhelmed by all this attention, I reckon."

"Don't let it go to your head," Hilda said, her tone pragmatic. "Of course, you will stay at Bayou le Jardin as our guest until you are feeling better. Both you and Josh."

"That's mighty nice, but we're not invalids. And we do have to get back to work."

"Just for a few more days," Hilda replied, the words a statement, not a request. "We're going to have a special church service this coming Sunday to thank the good Lord for all His blessings. And I want you and Josh to attend as our very special guests."

Mick couldn't turn down a request like that. "Yes, ma'am," he said, smiling slightly at the petite but formidable woman seated next to him. Then, because he had been hit on the head and he was still feeling a bit tilted, he asked, "Miss Hilda, do you believe in miracles, in divine intervention?"

"I most certainly do," she replied, tapping her elaborately carved cane against the linoleum floor. "Don't you?"

Mick couldn't tell her that he'd always considered his faith lackluster—a haphazard, halfhearted attempt at grasping for something, someone to guide him. But he could tell her about what had happened down in that building—something he'd refused to share with a roomful of reporters. "I don't know—I just felt this presence when I went in after Josh and Kathryn. It was almost as if someone were talking to me, guiding me. Whatever happened, it gave me the strength to come up out of there alive, and bring Josh and Kathryn with me."

"God was there with you, Mr. Love," Hilda replied with complete confidence.

Mick nodded, lowered his head a bit. "How can I be sure?"

"How can you doubt?" Hilda retorted, but the words were gentle. "You had no way of knowing this, but we were all praying after you went down there." She smiled at him, took his hand in hers. "We held hands—Lacey and Lorna and I—and we prayed. Then when we opened our eyes, we saw others doing the same thing." She let go of his hand and wagged a finger at him. "Never underestimate the power of positive prayer, Mr. Love."

"I won't," Mick told her, his words full of awe. "Not ever again."

Hilda patted his hand, then leaned on her cane to get up. Mick helped her with a hand on her arm. Then she turned to him, her smile a bit bemused. "You and my niece seem to have hit it off quite well, Mr. Love."

"Call me Mick," he said, wondering how to respond to her pointed comment.

"Then call me Aunt Hilda," she replied. "Everyone does." She leaned forward, propping her weight on her cane. "And tell me what's brewing between my Lorna and you."

Mick glanced around, as hot and uncomfortable as a crawfish about to hit a pot of boiling water. He didn't really have the answer to that particular question yet. But he was sure going to work on it. Yet what could he tell Aunt Hilda, to assure her he had only the most noble of intentions?

"I like Lorna a lot," he admitted. "She's..."

"Stubborn, opinionated, ornery, a challenge?" Hilda finished the statement, then waited, a serene smile on her peaches-and-cream face.

"All of the above," Mick said, laughing in spite of feeling like a trapped animal. "Lorna seems to have many layers—she's an independent woman who has a good career, and she loves her family. She works hard, that's for sure. And she seems to care deeply about the people she loves and the things she believes in."

"Sometimes too deeply," Hilda said, wagging her finger at him again. "I only ask that you remember that."

"I will," he said, nodding. "I wouldn't do anything to hurt Lorna, Aunt Hilda. You have my word on that."

"I'd expect nothing less," Hilda replied. "Now, what do you say we go and check on our patients? I'm anxious to talk to Kathryn and find out why she went into that building in the first place."

Mick offered his arm to Hilda. "Shall we?"

He was anxious, too. Anxious to find Lorna and get back to the unsettled business between them. Yet he couldn't put Aunt Hilda's warning out of his mind. Was that the reason Lorna seemed to be pushing him away, because she didn't want to care about him too much?

Was that the reason he saw that fear in her eyes each time he came near her?

Two days later, Mick's team had finished removing all the tree limbs and debris from the Bayou le Jardin property, and had managed to get the grounds back in shape enough to suit even the picky Mr. Justin Hayes. While Mick and Josh supervised from the sidelines—Hilda Dorsette and her two adorable nieces refused to let them actually do any work—Lucas and Justin both pitched in to help the men get the rest of the job done.

Then Claude Juneau, Mick's friend from the power company, came by to give Hilda a progress report on things in town, and to check on Mick and Josh. "Well, the National Guard and the Red Cross will both be pulling out today," said Claude, a giant man with bright red hair and ruddy cheeks, as they sat on the gallery enjoying the gloaming at the end of a long, warm spring day.

"The National Guard arrived right after the cavein the other day—too late to prevent that, but they did help remove most of the debris, and they gave us some much-needed relief in patrolling for looters. And the Red Cross has been great, but they've got other places to see about. Basically, now it's on to rebuilding and getting things back to normal, dealing with the insurance people, things such as that. Reckon we're on our own from here on out.''

Then he turned to Mick. ''Unless, of course, I could entice Mick here to keep his crew with us for a few more days. We could sure use some strong hands to finish the cleanup, and there's still some fallen trees that need to be removed mainly between here and town, just so we don't let them rot where they fell. We'd pay you for your efforts, of course.''

Mick glanced over at Josh, who sat on a cushioned wrought-iron love seat, right next to where Kathryn had her broken leg—straight from being set in the cast she'd have to wear for six weeks—propped on a pillow-laden footstool.

''Josh, what's on the agenda for the next week or so?''

Josh grinned, then squinted. ''Well, boss, let's see. We've got the Duvall's pines to trim back—that'll be about a week's worth of hard time. You know how Mrs. Duvall likes to supervise things. Then after that, it's just some odds and ends. A few clearings here and there around Vicksburg. We did hire on to clear away some dead oaks right outside Battleground Park, but that's not scheduled until later in the summer.'' He waved a hand at Mick. ''Besides, why am I telling you all of this? You know better than me what we've got on the agenda.''

Mick grinned. ''Just wanted to see if you'd jump right in and volunteer to stick around here for a few more days." He looked over at Kathryn, then shrugged.

Kathryn's smile gave him his answer, even if Josh didn't have the guts to say what was on his mind.

"That would be nice," she said, turning to glance over at Josh. "Especially since Aunt Hilda insisted I stay here until I'm feeling better."

"Only right," Hilda interjected. "Your momma has her hands full with your siblings and her grandchildren as it is. And besides, we can get some work done if you're handy."

Kathryn only nodded, then giggled again. "Leave it to you to be practical about all of this. But you're right, of course."

Aunt Hilda had also been right about Kathryn and Josh. Since the accident, they'd stuck together like glue to paper. Josh had stayed near Kathryn while she rested in the hospital, then had insisted on going with Aunt Hilda and Lacey to pick her up this afternoon.

Mick couldn't blame his friend, since he himself wanted to stick around to be near Lorna. And Josh certainly deserved some happiness in his life.

Kathryn was a pretty woman, no doubt. Her cropped black curls complimented the classic lines of her dark face, and her big round brown eyes opened even wider each time Josh talked, as if she couldn't get enough of all his wisdom. Each time she giggled at some brilliant remark coming from Josh's mouth, her large silver hoop earrings swayed against her slender neck. Broken leg or not, the woman seemed in very good spirits since the hospital had released her this morning.

And so did his friend, in spite of the stitches lining his back and arm. Maybe love was the best medicine, after all.

Which again brought Mick to his own need to stay at Bayou le Jardin a while longer.

Lorna Dorsette.

She was missing from this little circle.

She was back at her restaurant—which had re-opened today—no doubt fussing over the *potée* (some sort of salad), the *soufflé au fromage*, (it was made with cheese, from what he could tell), her *baguette* and *petit Parisien* breads, and his favorite, *brioche*, not to mention the bouillabaisse, the *homard à l'Americaine* (lobster with a tasty sauce), or the *caneton aux navets* (roasted duck) or the plain ol' *boeuf à la mode* (stuffed shrimp and pot roast) that the Garden Restaurant offered as entrees.

In fact, Lorna had been so busy, Mick had hardly had two minutes alone with her since the accident, but he'd sure learned a lot about French cooking. Maybe because he'd gone in the restaurant each night to stare at the menu when he wasn't watching her. If he kept this up, he'd gain ten pounds.

Lorna only ignored him and attended her other customers.

But he intended to fix that little oversight.

"We'll be glad to stay on," he told Claude now. "Besides, we promised Aunt Hilda we'd be in church this Sunday, and I don't think she'd take it too well if we up and left before then."

"I certainly would not," Hilda said, her eyes twinkling. "Lacey has told everyone in town to be there, so we can celebrate together. And I know Lorna has been issuing orders to Rosie Lee about what foods to prepare. We're going to have an old-fashioned dinner right here on the grounds after the service."

"I'll be there myself," Claude said, rubbing his broad stomach. "I'm telling you, Mick, when the Dorsette women put on a spread, a man never walks away hungry."

"All the more reason to stick around," Mick told his friend. "Oh, and Claude, I'm only going to charge you half rates for the work."

Claude reached out to shake his hand. "You're a good man, Mick. But then, I always did know that for a fact."

"How'd you two meet, anyway?" Lucas asked. He was sitting off to the side, out underneath one of the towering oaks, in a wooden glider, a boot propped against one arm of the swing while he slowly rocked himself back and forth with the other foot.

Mick looked over at Lucas. Now, there was a man who was very hard to read. From all indications, Lucas took life easy, showing up now and then to do some hard work, then disappearing for hours on end—to fiddle and play, Lacey seemed to think. But Mick knew better.

Tobbie had confided in Mick just this morning, telling him how much Lucas had helped with the cleanup around Tobbie's own modest home—which had suffered severe damage in the storm. Then Lucas had gone into the swamp to check up on the other Cajun families living there—families, Tobbie had said under his breath, that didn't have two nickels to rub together.

"They depend on Lucas's good graces," Rosie Lee had added. "But he don't like to brag about stuff like that."

Mick only knew Lucas always seemed to be around at the most crucial of times, like the other morning when he'd helped pull all three of them from the rubble. He'd pitched right in, taking over for Mick when the Dorsette women had insisted Mick and Josh take things easy. And Lucas had stepped in several times, intervening between Mick's crew and Justin Hayes, saving the day with some sort of humor to break the tension of too many chiefs trying to get things done.

Mick trusted Lucas. He didn't mind answering his question, either. "I met Claude when I used to work at the power company over in Jackson."

"He was young and hotheaded," Claude interjected, "so he didn't last very long."

Mick shrugged. "Long enough to know I liked working with trees. So I learned everything I could, took some college and technical courses, and I opened my own tree service—after a few years of false starts and several different jobs.''

"We kept in touch,'' Claude said by way of an explanation. "I kinda had to look out for him, you know. Didn't want him to do anything stupid.''

"He preached to me day and night,'' Mick said, laughing.

"Well, did any of it soak in?'' Claude asked, his big hands on his hips.

"Some,'' Mick replied. "At least, you managed to get me to come here. And I don't regret that at all.''

"Well, good. That's good.'' Claude raised a hand in the air. "Folks, I'd love to stay and chat, but I've got work to do, and since my wife and kids haven't seen me for three days, I'd better get home before the sun goes down.''

"Thank you for coming out, Claude,'' Lacey said from the open doorway leading to the kitchen.

"No problem.'' Then Claude turned to Mick again. "See you first thing in the morning, then?''

"We'll be there,'' Mick told him. "Josh can supervise, while the rest of us work.''

They followed Claude to his truck, then Josh punched Mick on the arm. "So, I guess this means we're all sticking around for a spell.''

"I guess it does, at that,'' Mick replied. "I'll go down to the cottages and tell the rest of the crew, then I'll call our secretary back home and let her know to hold off on any more appointments.''

They all looked up to see Lorna hurrying up the path from the restaurant, her blue linen dress kicking up with each quick step she took. She was wearing her white chef coat over the dress and a prim white kerchief scarf on her head, keeping her long hair away from her face.

''We keep blowing fuses,'' she said immediately. ''The lights keep dimming, and the stove goes on and off.'' Lacey shot out the door. ''But you're not in complete darkness, right.''

Lorna held up a small flashlight. ''No. It's okay.'' Mick noticed the long look passing between the sisters before Lorna said, ''But I'm going to have that electrician's head on a platter. He assured me it was safe to go ahead and open up today.''

Lucas let out a hoot of laughter. ''You tell 'em, Sister Lorna.''

Lorna whirled on her brother. ''And you, just sitting there as if you don't have a care in the world—''

''I don't,'' Lucas replied, saluting her with one hand to his temple. ''I'm sorry. Did you need something?''

''I could use some help,'' she replied, her green eyes flashing like heat lightning. ''Believe it or not, we have a large crowd tonight, and one of my waiters couldn't make it in—he's still dealing with losing part of his roof to the storm.''

Lucas hopped up, brushed his hands on his faded jeans. "Okay, I'll wait tables, but only if you let me play a few tunes when things settle down. I'm in a blues kinda mood."

"Fine, work first, then play that whining saxophone later—just so my customers are happy."

With that, she stomped right past Mick and into the kitchen, leaving a scent of fresh herbs and floral perfume to merge in his head.

But they could still hear her ranting, her hands in the air. "I had to go for a walk, or lose it in front of all my employees and the customers. Plus, in all of the clutter and confusion, we seem to have misplaced at least half of our measuring bowls. I'm going to borrow a couple from the kitchen."

"She is very precise about these things," Lucas said, before heading off in a lazy stroll toward the restaurant. Walking backward, he directed his next words to Mick.

"Has to have everything in order, just for good measure, of course, or so she tells us."

Lacey watched her brother grin, then pivot toward the lane with an eloquent parting shrug. "That man never gets in a hurry about anything. Honestly, I just don't get my brother at all."

Hilda hushed her. "Lucas knows his own mind, and he knows when he's needed and when he's not."

"So, leave him alone, right?" Lacey didn't look

too pleased, but she quieted under her aunt's warning glance.

"Yes, leave him alone. He's never let any of us down, has he?"

"Well, no." Lacey lowered her head. "I guess we're just all a bit frazzled. This has been one long, busy week."

"All the more reason to rest and rejoice come Sunday," Hilda replied. "Now, children, I'm rather tired. I'm going to take my supper on a tray in my room, look over some files, then go to bed." She gave Kathryn a pointed look. "And I suggest you do the same, young lady. That pain medicine should be kicking in soon."

"Yes, ma'am," Kathryn said quietly. Then she added, "I'm sorry I caused everybody such a scare. But I could hear that little kitty meowing..."

Her voice trailed off as her eyes misted over with tears. Josh took her hand, his own eyes going soft. "You sure were brave."

Aunt Hilda nodded, her eyes misty, too. "Yes, and we're very glad the kitten, the child, and all of the rest of you are safe and sound."

Everyone fell silent for a minute, then Aunt Hilda said, "Now, I'm off to get to that paperwork."

Mick got up when Aunt Hilda rose. "Do you need help getting up those stairs?"

Hilda chuckled. "I have my own elevator in the back of the house, Mick. I didn't want the thing installed, but actually it's come in quite handy, especially since I have arthritis in my bad knee. It even has a nice bench seat, so I can sit as I ride up. But thanks for the gentlemanly offer, anyway.''

"My pleasure,'' Mick said. "I don't remember seeing an elevator,'' he told Lacey, after Hilda had gone inside.

"It's hidden from the public,'' she explained. "It's behind the back stairway, near the kitchen. Guests never wander that far back, and it's rather nondescript so no one will notice it—it looks like another door.''

"I see.'' Another of the many interesting stories surrounding this old house.

But Mick wasn't worried about elevators right now. He wanted to talk to Lorna. Glancing down at Josh, he asked, "Friend, will you be all right? I think I'll go for a walk before supper—get some of the kinks out of this sore body.''

"We'll be just fine,'' Josh replied, his eyes on Kathryn. "I'll make sure Kat gets tucked in, then I'm going to bed myself. These stitches are starting to burn.''

Kathryn slapped him playfully on his good arm, before batting her thick, dark lashes at him. "I'm gonna have to check in with my momma. She'll be worried if I don't call.''

Mick pointed to Josh. "And she should be, if you're gonna keep hanging around with this one.''

But he grinned when he said it, and Kathryn only giggled again.

It was downright sickening to see Josh and Kathryn so wrapped up in each other, but Mick couldn't begrudge his friend this chance at love.

Only, he wanted that same chance with Lorna. And it didn't help matters one bit when he reminded himself that he'd vowed to steer clear of any binding relationships, that he'd learned his lesson with Melinda, that he wasn't worth the dirt underneath Lorna Dorsette's pretty feet.

None of those warnings or reminders could stop him from achieving his purpose for being here. A purpose he somehow knew he'd regret in the long run.

But he needed to test that purpose, needed to find out if what he'd been feeling was real or imagined, if all of this disaster and drama had heightened the attraction, or if the attraction had been real from the first time he'd touched her.

Which is why he marched into the kitchen to find Lorna. She might be busy, but Mick intended to make his presence known.

And he intended to take up right where he'd left off yesterday. He wanted another kiss, just for good measure.

Chapter Nine

"You sure are making a lot of noise," Mick told Lorna a few minutes later.

She whirled around, inhaled deeply, then tried to ignore the feathering of butterflies hopelessly trapped in her stomach. But how could she ignore the effect this man had on her? Or the lasting impression his kiss had left in her heart and head?

She was certainly going to give it her best shot.

"Found them," she said, holding up two big glass mixing bowls. "Got to get back to the restaurant."

"Just hold on a minute," he said, reaching out to catch her arm, as she tried to slip by.

From her spot at the stove, Rosie Lee cast them an amused look, then quickly brought her gaze back to the pork roast she'd prepared for dinner.

But Lorna knew exactly what her friend was thinking. Not wanting to give Rosie Lee the satisfaction of witnessing one of her tirades, Lorna glanced down at Mick's hand. "I have to get back—"

"Okay, then, I'll walk with you."

He took the bowls right out of her arms. "Busy night, huh?"

"Ah, yes." She had no choice but to start walking. "Don't you want to stay and sample Rosie Lee's pork roast with lemon pepper?"

"Save me a bite, will you, Rosie Lee?" he said over his shoulder.

"Of course," Rosie Lee answered. Lorna didn't miss the slight smile curving the woman's lips.

"Really, Mick, I can carry those myself. Stay here and enjoy your dinner with the family."

"I'd rather walk with you. Nice night, don't you think?"

Lorna decided he wasn't going to take no for an answer, so she had to be polite, at least. She'd tried really hard to avoid him these past few days, but it hadn't been easy. He'd shown up at the restaurant every night, sitting there with a menu in front of him as his gaze followed her. Mick had become a loyal customer.

If she didn't at least talk to him, he'd probably spend another evening sampling way too much French cuisine. So she answered his question with politeness and grace, hoping those two attributes would hide her agitation and agony. "Yes, it's a bit warm, but nice. The gardens are looking much better, though, thanks to your crew.''

''Yeah, the mud's dried up and everything is getting back into shape. We talked with the landscaper earlier today. He's already getting new flowers in place. Seems to have a lot of nervous energy, that one.''

''Justin is a hard worker,'' Lorna replied, glad to be talking about a safe, comfortable subject such as gardening. ''And he has a major crush on Lacey.''

''Oh, really?''

''They've known each other for years, since we came here. But I don't think she's interested. They're good friends, though.''

''You Dorsette women tend to have a lot of men friends, I do believe.''

They were nearing the summerhouse now, which only made Lorna remember being there with him the other morning. She also remembered how she'd lashed out at him. Obviously, he wasn't holding that against her anymore. But she didn't want to bring up their gentle truce or the kiss or anything else between them, so she decided to talk about her sister, instead.

''Lacey was married once.''

That turned his head. ''I didn't know.''

''She doesn't talk about it much. Neil was a pilot in the Air Force. His plane crashed on a routine training mission.''

Mick stopped her, a hand once again on her arm. "I'm sorry to hear that."

There was more to the story, but Lorna wouldn't share that with him. Lacey wouldn't want his pity. "Now, when people call her Lacey Dorsette, she doesn't bother to correct them. But her actual name is Lacey Dorsette York."

"How long ago did this happen?"

"Oh, it's been about six years. They were stationed up in Shreveport at Barksdale. She came home to Bayou le Jardin immediately after it happened. Neil is buried in our family plot at the chapel."

And my sister has retreated behind a wall of sadness and duty, she wanted to add.

"Well, that is a tragedy," Mick said, as they started back down the path toward the restaurant. "But who knows, maybe this friendship between her and Justin will turn into something more."

"Maybe, but I doubt it," Lorna replied. "Lacey is too afraid to let go of her heart again."

"And what about her little sister?"

The question threw her so off-kilter, she almost stumbled. "What do you mean?"

Mick halted again. Balancing the mixing bowls against his hip, he said, "I think you know what I mean, Lorna. What about you? What about us? Are we just friends, or did that kiss change things between us? Are *you* willing to let go of your heart?"

Too many questions, coming at her much too fast.

Lorna glanced down the path toward the noise and lights of her beloved restaurant. Longing to run to the safety of bubbling stews and hot ovens, she swallowed back the fear that choked at her, determined to be honest with Mick. Well, almost honest.

"There is no 'us,' Mick. We just got carried away the other day."

"Yeah, you could say that. And I guess I should say I won't let it happen again—only, I want it to happen again."

She wouldn't look at him. Couldn't. "It can't happen again."

But he made her look. He moved ahead of her until he was in her direct view, his face blocking out her escape route. "Why can't it?"

Lorna finally lifted her gaze to his face. "Because...I'm through wandering around. And you're apparently not. I came home to find some peace, some purpose in my life. And I'm content, living here, working here." The explanation sounded feeble, but it was the only one she could give him right now.

"What's that got to do with us?"

She threw up her hands, then let them drop to her sides. "Isn't that obvious? You like traveling around, doing your job. I can respect that, since I used to be filled with wanderlust myself. But I can't live like that anymore, and I won't ask you to become tied down—not when we've only just met and...this whole situation has gotten way out of hand."

"What situation?"

She moaned, expelled a breath. "Us."

"I thought you said there was no 'us.'"

"You known what I mean, Mick."

He lowered his head, bringing his face to within inches of hers. "I think I get it. You're afraid of what you're feeling for me because you think I'll be gone soon."

She shrugged, hoping to sound nonchalant. "Maybe."

"Is that what always happened before, in your other relationships?"

Lorna wanted to laugh. If he only knew. But she couldn't tell him that before, she'd always been the one to run away first—that is, until Cole had left her standing at the altar. Just when someone started getting close, or wanted more of a commitment, she got cold feet and broke things off, or worse, just up and left, like the coward she was. Cole had figured it all out, though. And he'd left her because he couldn't deal with her terrors in the night.

What if Mick reacted the same way?

This time, it was different. This time, she couldn't run. But Mick could easily walk away once he realized she was a coward, once he saw her for what she really was.

"Answer me, Lorna," he said, his hand settling on her hair. "Is that why you won't let me get any closer?"

"That's part of it," she replied, moving away to start toward the restaurant.

"And what's the other part?" he said behind her. "What's really going on here, Lorna?" When she hesitated, he asked, "Is it because of what I said the other day in the summerhouse? Because I grew up poor, living in a trailer park?"

She whirled around, shock filtering through her resistance. "Don't be ridiculous. Contrary to what you might think, I'm not a snob. And believe me, until Aunt Hilda took us in, we lived in much worse conditions than a trailer park. We lived in a hut in the jungle, with snakes and scorpions and spiders..." She stopped, dread and fear making her feel weak at the knees. Unable to look at him, she lowered her head. "I'm not that way, Mick."

Mick lifted her head with a finger under her chin, his face full of curiosity and questions. But thankfully, he didn't ask. Instead, he said, "I'm sorry. But I had to know. I'm not proud of my background, Lorna, and I could certainly understand if—"

"It's not that," she interrupted as she drew her chin away from his touch. "This is happening too fast, Mick. Can't you see that? Can't you understand that I've never—"

She paused, turned away again.

"Never what? Felt like this before?" he asked, following right on her heels. "'Cause that's the way I'm feeling. Like I've been hit by lightning."

"Or lived through a storm," she said, almost to herself. That's exactly what it felt like, being with him, being in his arms, as if she were reliving the storm all over again—helpless, frightened, alone in the dark.

"Lorna?"

They were at the door of the restaurant now. From inside, Lorna heard the sweet, sad notes of her brother's saxophone drifting out over the night. Lucas was such a paradox. Only her brother could play gospel songs on the saxophone and make people want to get down on their knees and praise the Lord, even if they felt the blues all the way to their toes. "Shall We Gather at the River" had never sounded so poignant, so clear.

Lorna wanted to sit down and cry. It was so tempting to do just that, to sit down and pour her heart out in a good old-fashioned sobbing fit.

But Mick was there, waiting. And she couldn't allow him to see her pain or her confusion. Or her tears.

"Lorna?" he asked again. "Can we talk about this?"

"I have to get back," she said, her head down.

"Then later. Meet me in the summerhouse after you're done here. Please?"

Her heart hammered a warning, reminding her of the beat of a drum somewhere in that faraway jungle. "We don't close until eleven."

"I'll wait."

Her head reeled at the prospect of walking back up the path alone to meet him there in the darkened summerhouse, causing her to close her eyes for just a second. "I could be awfully late."

"I don't care. I don't think I'll get much sleep, anyway."

You don't understand, she wanted to shout. *I can't meet you there. It's so very dark there late at night. How can I make you understand?*

But Lorna couldn't bring herself to confess her frightening secret to Mick. What if he, too, shunned her, laughed at her silliness the way so many others had done before? Walked away out of frustration the way Cole had done? No, she couldn't bear that. Not this time. And yet, this time she couldn't run away, either. But she had to convince him, somehow, that she wasn't worth his time or his energy.

"Don't wait for me, Mick. I have a lot to do tonight."

He leaned close, then shoved the bowls into her hands, his blue eyes turning to black in the growing dusk. "I said I don't care. I'll be there. And I expect you to show up."

Then he turned and left her standing at the door of the restaurant, while the notes of the saxophone filled the night around her with a misty fog of regret and rejoicing.

"Ready to go home now?" Lucas asked Lorna hours later.

Lorna lifted her tired eyes from the computer, then hit the save button on the bookkeeping program. Glancing up at the clock, she was surprised to see that it was well after midnight. "I didn't realize how late it was," she told her brother as she pivoted in the swivel chair.

"I'm sorry I made you hang around all night."

Lucas gave her a grin, then reached out to pull her hair, just as he'd often done when they were growing up. "Didn't mind one bit, sis. It gave me a chance to play some of my tunes."

She got up, stretched, then laughed. "The customers always enjoy your impromptu shows. And I think they especially needed to hear some good music tonight."

Lucas ran a hand down his beard stubble, then did a little spin toward her. "And I think my baby sister needed to hear some good tunes herself. What's up with you and the tree expert, anyway?"

Knowing she couldn't hide anything from Lucas, Lorna sank back down in her chair. The little office off the back of the kitchen was quiet now. All the employees had gone home, and everything was neat and tidy, ready for tomorrow, just the way Lorna liked it. They'd had a fairly large crowd, considering the entire town was still dealing with the aftereffects of the tornado. But then, she reminded herself, the place always drew a large crowd from Kenner, too. Lots of folks had come just to see how much storm damage Bayou le Jardin had suffered.

Finally, she looked up at her brother. He waited patiently, letting her take her time in answering his question. At times such as this, she loved that about Lucas. He never hurried anything.

"I don't know what's going on between Mick and me," she admitted. "He kissed me the other day, after the cave-in."

Lucas swung his lithe body up onto a nearby credenza, then settled back against the wall, his black eyes regarding her with a curious intensity.

"That cave-in must have been mighty powerful. First Josh and Kathryn, and now you and our Mr. Love. I guess a life-or-death experience can do that for a person."

"We should know, right?" Lorna replied softly.

"Yeah." Lucas looked away then, his eyes turning a shade of midnight that Lorna recognized. The memories of their parents' death always did that—made them turn away and retreat into their own nightmares. But Lucas didn't stay in that distant horror long. "So, he kissed you? What's the big deal? You've been kissed before, right?"

"Right." Lorna pushed at the loose curls falling away from her braid. "I don't know, Lucas. I don't know if it was all the excitement of the accident and the rescue, or if Mick and I really are attracted to each other. I only know that it scared me."

"Different than the rest, hmm, *petite fleur?*"

"*Oui,*" Lorna responded, lapsing into the French they sometimes used when they didn't want others to know what they were saying. Although they were very much alone, Lorna didn't want Mick to walk in and hear them discussing him. "*Mais, sa c'est fou!*"

"Now why is that so crazy?" Lucas asked, leaning his head down, his dark eyes widening. "Don't you deserve to feel some *joie de vie?*"

Lorna got up, started putting files away. "That's the crazy part. Kissing Mick did bring me joy—such immense joy that I don't know how to deal with it. I only just met the man—how can I feel this way? How?"

Lucas hopped off the credenza to stand in front of her. Looking down at her, he put a hand on each of her arms. "I don't have an answer for that, *chère*. But I do have some advice."

"I could use some of that."

"Go with it, love. Let it happen. Stop fighting against your heart. Lorna, you are a beautiful woman with a big heart and a soul that needs to be filled with love. Don't run from that."

Lorna groaned, then slapped him away. "Some help you are. You have a poet's soul, Lucas, and you fall in love at the drop of a hat. How am I supposed to trust anything you tell me?"

"Good point." His grin was full of the old charm.

"But hey, I enjoy life to the fullest. I have fun. Why can't you and Lacey do that?"

"Because we have other things to consider," she told him as she turned out the lights and, flashlight in hand and on full blast, headed for the back door. "We have responsibilities, duties, obligations."

"I have all of those things, too," Lucas told her, turning to make sure everything was locked up tight before they headed up the path toward the mansion. "I know neither of you think that, but I am dedicated to this family."

"We understand that," Lorna replied. "It's just easier for you, I guess."

"Falling in love is never easy," he replied. "The hard part is falling out of love. When it's over, it's over. And it's sometimes hard to face."

"You don't seem to have a problem with that."

"I'm the shallow one, remember," he said, his voice going quiet again. "But let's get back to you. So what do you intend to do about Mr. Love?"

Lorna looked out at the night looming before them. Was Mick still there, waiting in the summerhouse?

"I don't know," she said on a whisper. "He wants me to meet him in the summerhouse. He told me he'd wait until I came up the path."

Lucas did a slow dance around her, smiling. "Well, that would be right about now, don't you think?"

"I'm frightened," she told him.

"You have your flashlight," Lucas said, coming

close in an automatic gesture of protection. "And you have me. I'll escort you there myself."

They started toward the summerhouse together.

"It's not the dark so much—I'm afraid of my feelings for Mick."

"I can help there, too. If he gets too pushy."

Lorna tugged her brother close. "Don't worry, Mick is a perfect gentleman. But thanks for the chivalrous offer. I don't know what I'd do without you."

"Just remember that," he teased as he took her by the hand. "Right now, you need to find your suitor, though. Can't leave a man waiting too long, darlin'."

"I suppose that's an expert opinion."

"I am the expert on love," he replied, winking. "Even if my last name isn't Love."

They were approaching the summerhouse. Lorna could see the white outline of the building in the muted moonlight. The curtains billowed out in the wind, beckoning her to come inside.

"Full moon," Lucas commented, whistling low. "The gardens are shimmering with it."

"At least, I have that to be thankful about," she replied, her hands sweaty, her steps unsure.

"You have a lot to be thankful about, *belle*. Don't forget that."

"You're right," Lorna said, nodding. "Maybe I should take your advice and just enjoy myself for a change."

"There you go," Lucas said, pointing to a shadow

inside the circular building. "Want me to check it out, make sure it's safe?"

But Lucas didn't get a chance to do that. Mick must have heard them coming up the path. He came to one of the open doors, leaning a shoulder against the frame as he watched them—watched Lorna—approach.

Even in the muted light, Lorna knew it was him. She could see the stark white patch of his bandaged forehead, and she could feel his eyes on her.

"Mick, what a pleasant surprise," Lucas said, all exaggeration. "Enjoying the moonlight?"

"Very much," Mick answered, his hands tucked in the pockets of his jeans, his eyes still on Lorna.

Lorna turned to her brother. "Thanks for walking me home, Lucas. I'll see you in the morning."

"Are you sure?" Lucas waited, fully prepared to stick around if Lorna needed him.

"I'm sure. I'm okay, really," she said close to his ear. "The moonlight helps."

Lucas gave his sister a peck on the cheek, then turned to Mick. "Will you make sure she gets in the house safely?"

Lorna didn't miss the brotherly protection in that question, and apparently neither did Mick.

"I'll be glad to," Mick replied. "Don't worry."

Lucas shrugged. "Me, never." Then he turned, waved, and said, "Don't keep her out too late."

"I won't," Mick replied. Then after Lucas had

strolled on up the path, he added, "Your brother sure is protective."

"That's what brothers are for," Lorna told him, her nerves thrashing like loose bramble inside her body as she glanced over his clean T-shirt and faded jeans.

"I guess I don't blame him," Mick replied, still leaning against the door frame.

She couldn't explain that Lucas knew her deepest pain and her worst secrets, and that because he was her brother, he would hold both close to his heart unless she told him otherwise. And so would Lacey. Lorna returned their trust in the same way. It had always been that way among the three of them. She doubted Mick would understand that kind of bond, forged out of terror on a dark, storm-tossed night so long ago.

"I didn't think you would come," Mick told her, bringing her back to this fragrant, moon-washed summerhouse.

"I wasn't going to," she replied.

"Why did you?"

She shrugged, her voice lifting into a question. "It was on the way?"

"Not good enough." He tugged her close. "You came because you feel the same way I do. Because you know in your heart there is an 'us.'"

Lorna resisted his touch, resisted the soapy-clean smell of his hair, resisted the warmth that wrapped around her like a security blanket, blocking out the darkness and all her fears. "Maybe I came because I wanted to convince you that you're wrong."

"I'm not wrong—not this time."

And that was what she feared the most.

"How can you be so sure? You'll be gone in a few days. You'll probably leave right after church on Sunday."

Mick gathered her into his embrace, his face inches from hers. "Now that's where *you're* wrong. Claude Juneau came by today, asked me and the crew to hire on and help him clear up a few more trouble spots. I told him we'd stay."

Lorna felt the breath leaving her body, like a river tide being pulled away from the shore. "You're staying?"

"That's what I just told you."

His head dipped. His lips touched her cheekbone, making it extremely hard for her to focus, to concentrate. "For how long?"

He moved his mouth over her face in little feathery kisses that made her think of a soft field of clover. "Well, now, that just depends, don't you think?"

"Depends?" She tried to find her breath. Tried to find some reasoning thought. "On what?"

"On you," he said.

His lips cut off any kind of response she might have offered—except for the soft moan that escaped as she fell against him and gave in to his sweet, reassuring kiss.

Chapter Ten

Mick didn't want the kiss to end. But before he took this any further, he had to tell Lorna a few things. About him. About his past.

So he pulled away from her, then stood back to stare down at her. She looked so young and innocent, standing there, colored all lavender and blue in the moonlight. The scent of night-blooming jasmine and honeysuckle surrounded her as if she were a natural part of this garden. And he supposed she was.

Longing to ask her what had happened to her parents, why she'd lived in a jungle, why she and her siblings were so protective and close, he instead just stood there looking at her. He didn't want to frighten her away with too many probing questions. Not yet. Right now, he wanted to memorize her face, her lips, her smile.

Just in case she turned away from him.

"We need to talk," he said at last, his voice husky from need, his emotions lifting and scattering like the curtains that billowed out all around them.

He saw her nod, watched as she pushed a hand through the loose curls at her forehead.

"Lorna, I don't have a whole lot to offer a woman. I have a nice enough house back in Vicksburg. I built it on a bluff, thinking I'd get married and raise my children there. But my fiancée decided she didn't want to stay there waiting on me to come home after a long job. We were engaged, had been for about a year. I'd just finished the house, when she told me, standing in the middle of the empty living room, that she'd fallen in love with someone else. Someone who could provide her with a comfortable living, someone who could be there when she came home at night. Someone who didn't like to wander around the way I did."

Mick saw the surprise rushing like the humid wind over Lorna's face.

"You were engaged?" The question held a hint of hurt, of regret.

"Yep. Didn't work out, though. And I've been traveling ever since. I decided maybe she was right, maybe I didn't need to settle down, after all."

"She…she married someone else?"

He nodded, his laughter low and harsh. "My best friend."

"What?"

"The man who helped me build the house. While I was out making a living to pay for the thing, he and Melinda got very close. I can't say that I blame them. They were together so much, going over the plans, working on the house day and night. It was bound to happen, I guess."

"Not if she really loved you."

Mick heard the soft, fierce tenderness in that declaration. It went straight to his heart. "Then I guess she didn't really love me. And I guess I didn't love her enough to go back and fight for her."

"So you just walked away, let your friend take her?"

"Yes, that's exactly what I did. I didn't have much faith in anything back then. Not her, certainly not myself."

"And what about your faith in God?"

That wasn't what he'd expected, but then, this was Lorna, after all. He smiled, then shrugged. "I guess that was pretty weak, too. In fact, it's been that way for a while now. Until I came here."

"Here?" She lifted her chin a notch, her green eyes shimmering like forbidden emeralds caught in a beam of moonlight. "You mean, Bayou le Jardin has strengthened your faith in God?"

He wanted her to understand that he'd never felt this way before. But how did he explain something so elusive? "From the first moment, I think," he began, his hands touching hers. "When you told me that God had sent me, I took it seriously."

"I believed it, too," she said, her fingers curling around his, warm and reassuring. "I was so frightened that night, during the storm. And when it was all over, I was so very thankful. I had to get away from all the noise, all the confusion, just to talk to God. And I did ask Him to send us help—not just for this place, but the whole town." Her expression was full of amazement. "And then you came."

"And then—"

"You saved me from that tree limb."

"I thought you were a little boy."

"I always was the tomboy."

"You're not a tomboy now, that's for sure, Lorna. You're all woman."

She laughed. "Maybe we'd better get back to your faith."

Mick wanted to get back to kissing her and holding her, but he needed to talk about this. It had been a very long time since he'd wanted to discuss religion with anyone. "It just seemed as if this peace came over me, holding you there in my arms. As if I'd finally come home." He shifted, pulled her with him to lean back against a support column. "Then when the building caved in, and I went in after Josh and Kathryn, I just knew—I was meant to be here, right here, for some reason."

"To save us."

"But I didn't save anyone. I just did what had to be done."

Lorna reached up to touch the bandage on his forehead. "But, Mick, think about it. What if you hadn't been here? You and Josh both? I might not be standing here right now, and Kathryn might be dead."

"I don't understand any of it," he admitted, "but I do know that something inside me changed when I went down in that building. I heard...I heard something, someone, telling me not to give up."

"So you felt closer to God?"

"Yes. And I still do. You know, my momma taught me the word of God, but I kinda just let it wash right over me."

Lorna moved her fingers down his face, making his heart hurt with need.

"Mick, when you thought God's word was washing right over you, it was really washing through you. You had the foundation and the knowledge—you just didn't know how to apply it."

Trust Lorna to make it all seem so simple. But it wasn't that simple. His life was changing right before his eyes, and Mick wasn't sure how to deal with that.

"Maybe you're right. I mean, you and your family have such a strong faith. It's impressive."

"We don't mean to impress. It's just the way we feel. It's the way we view the world."

"So you're completely confident in your faith?"

She dropped her hand, then moved away. Mick saw

the defensiveness in her gestures, in the way she put her arms against her stomach. "Most of the time, yes."

"But?"

"We all struggle with our faith at times, I suppose. But Aunt Hilda has taught us to trust in the Lord, to depend on Him in all things. When she's worried, she goes out into the garden and talks to God."

"That's not always easy."

"No, it's not. But my family and I know He's there. And He's here—" She reached a hand up to her heart.

"Do you think he brought us together?"

Mick saw her smile. It radiated from her face, lighting up the night. "I sure hope so."

"But you still have doubts?"

"Yes, I have to admit, I do. Especially after what you just told me about Melinda and your friend. I don't think you want to trust me, Mick."

"It's hard to trust after that, but it was my fault. I couldn't give Melinda what she wanted."

"A big house and lots of charge cards?"

"Yeah, and security. That's what she really wanted. She wanted someone she could count on."

"Don't we all?"

"And what if I can't give that to you, either? Do you think you can count on me? Do you think I can give you that kind of security?"

Lorna moved close again, then reached out a hand

to him. "Maybe it's not up to you to give me security. Maybe *I* just need to be secure enough to accept what you can offer me."

Mick held her hand up to his lips, kissing the delicate, slender fingers. "I told you, I don't *have* much to offer. At least, not compared to the life you have here."

"That's where you're wrong," she whispered.

Mick's lips moved from her hand to her mouth. He kissed her again, putting everything he wanted to give her into that one intimate gesture.

When he lifted his head, he said, "So...there is an 'us'? I mean, are you willing to explore the possibilities?"

She laid her head on his shoulder, then let out a deep sigh. "I don't know. I've had a lot of false starts, Mick. I've hurt people, and I've been hurt. And there's so much about me that you don't know, that I'm not ready to tell you." Raising her head, she glanced back up at him. "The Dorsettes are famous for falling in love too quickly, so I want to be very cautious with you."

"Why? Why not just go with how you feel?"

"I've done that before, and it's backfired. This time, I want to be completely sure."

Mick thought he knew why she was being so careful. "Maybe because of what I just told you? You said earlier that you're done with traveling around. You're settled here. But with me, well, you'd have to deal with my job, my long hours, lots of time away from home.''

''That's part of it,'' she told him. ''But I can live with that, I think. Right now, I just want to be sure about what I'm feeling. What it really means.''

Mick knew what it meant to him, having her in his arms. But he understood her doubts. He pulled her close again. ''We've got some time to consider all of that. Right now, *this* feels right.''

He held her there as they leaned against the ornate column, the moonlight and night breezes playing all around them, the scent of magnolias mixed with the rich distinct loam of the swamp surrounding them in a humid mist. Just outside the door, the white blossoms of a moon vine glistened and swayed, opening to follow the night.

Finally, Lorna shifted in his arms. ''It's getting late. And you promised to walk me to the door.''

''Do you have to go?''

''Yes. Tomorrow is another busy day. The restaurant really fills up.''

Reluctantly, he guided her through the dark, shadowy garden. He noticed that she kept her flashlight on and pointed ahead of them until they'd reached the lighted back gallery of the imposing house. ''Will you be okay from here, or do you want me to make sure you get to your room?''

''No, this is fine.'' She glanced toward the well-lit staircase, then turned the flashlight off. ''Mick, thank you for being honest with me. About your past, I mean.''

''I just wanted you to know.''

And he wanted to know all about her, too. When she was ready to tell him.

''Well, good night,'' she said, her tone making her sound shy.

''Lorna—'' He couldn't resist pulling her back into his arms for one more kiss.

''This is crazy,'' she said on a breathless whisper.

''We don't have to rush,'' he told her. ''I'll be around for a while longer. We can take it slow, get to know each other.''

''That would be nice.''

Then she slipped away from him like a dancer and moved inside. Mick watched through the glass doors as she headed upstairs.

For a very long time after that, he waited inside the summerhouse, remembering the feel of her in his arms, his gaze riveted on the light from her bedroom.

The light that never went out.

The next morning at dawn, Mick woke up in the cottage to that same light shining down from her window. Did Lorna stay up later than everyone else, then get up before the rest of the family? Or did she simply keep a light burning all night long? Sitting up in bed, he said, ''That's got to be it.''

Mick suddenly realized why he'd seen that fear and dread in Lorna's eyes so many times, and why Lucas had seemed so protective, why Laccy always asked if Lorna was all right. Why Lorna always carried a flashlight at night.

Quietly, so he wouldn't wake Josh and David, Mick got up and went outside to stand on the small cottage porch, his eyes never leaving Lorna's bedroom window.

"Lorna, are you afraid of the dark?"

That had to be it. She didn't like the darkness, didn't like being alone in the night.

If that was the truth, then Mick knew all of her insecurities had to be tied up in that one fear.

But why? What had caused her to be so afraid?

Lorna stood beside Mick in the tiny cedar-walled chapel located on the edge of the plantation grounds. Famous for the many weddings and christenings that were held here annually, the Chapel in the Garden was a quiet retreat that offered the Dorsette family and the entire community a place to worship in a peaceful, country setting.

The outside walls of the chapel had been built in 1850 out of cypress logs pulled from the nearby swamp, but it was now remodeled and painted a stark, glistening white. Square and compact with an ornate steeple complete with a brass bell, the small building couldn't hold a lot of people. But today it looked as if most of the townspeople had come to give thanks to God and celebrate with a dinner on the grounds back at the mansion.

Lorna was glad to see so many friends turning out for this special service. The town had survived the storm without any lives lost. Those who'd been injured were slowly recovering, and most of the cleanup was under control.

Now would come the rebuilding and the rejoicing.

She turned to look up at Mick. He was still here, but she knew he'd have to leave soon. He had worked so hard over the past few days, helping Claude to clear away the remaining debris and trees, helping Lucas and Justin get the gardens back in shape for the rest of the spring tourist season, doing whatever needed to be done, whether or not it involved his particular expertise. He'd sent some of his crew back to Vicksburg, but a couple of the men, along with Josh as supervisor while he was still recuperating from his wounds, had stayed to help out. Lorna would never forget their willingness to get the job done. Nor would she forget Mick's patience and understanding.

He'd gone out and worked each day, then returned to her each night. Their late-night meetings in the summerhouse had fueled the curiosity of both her family and the Babineaux.

Everyone wanted to know what was going on between Lorna and Mick.

She wished she could answer that particular question. After everything Mick had told her about his past, she now understood that he had come a long way. He'd found his way back to God, here in her gardens. He'd shared his journey with her, making her see that this hadn't been easy for him. Not after what had happened with Melinda and his friend. The woman he'd loved was now married to someone else; that had left Mick distrustful and doubtful.

Lorna knew that feeling, at least. And while she appreciated Mick's ability to open up and tell her the truth about his past, Lorna didn't know if she'd ever be able to do the same. And yet, she sensed Mick was waiting for just that. How long would he be willing to wait?

Lacey poked her, bringing Lorna's mind back to the song they were singing. As they finished the last verse of "Standing on the Promise," Lacey leaned over. "Where were you just then? Your lips weren't even moving to the music."

"Just thinking," Lorna replied, as they all settled back on the polished wooden church pews to listen to Reverend Mahoney's sermon.

"About *him?*" Lacey lifted a pink-polished fingernail toward Mick, her gaze on Lorna's face.

"Would you please stop pointing. It's rude," Lorna hissed back, hoping Mick hadn't seen Lacey.

"I'm not pointing, merely indicating," Lacey replied as she straightened the skirt of her light yellow cotton dress. "Aunt Hilda is concerned that you two are getting mighty close, mighty fast."

Lorna glanced up to where her aunt was sitting in front of them, wearing a white hat with a large yellow sunflower on its brim, Lucas right beside her in his tan summer suit and tie. Josh sat next to Lucas with Kathryn, who had her broken leg, cast and all, out in the aisle, while Kathryn's mother sat behind them next to Mick, keeping a close watch on her lovesick daughter.

Lorna studied her aunt, then put a hand over her mouth to talk to her sister. "She doesn't look concerned to me. In fact, she looks downright joyful."

"She's in church," Lacey retorted. "She always looks that way in church, whether she's worried or not."

"Well, she doesn't have to worry about me," Lorna said, her whisper lifting up in a muffled echo.

Lucas looked around, turned his head sideways, then brought a tanned finger to his smiling lips. "Shh."

Lorna gave her brother a nasty glare, then pushed at Lacey's hand on her arm. "Can we talk about this later?"

"Sure." Lacey settled back, her porcelain face all innocence, her glance cutting over Lorna to Mick. When he looked around, she smiled prettily, then pretended to be shuffling through the church bulletin in her hand.

"Everything okay?" Mick said in Lorna's ear, his warm breath reminding her of moonlight and kisses.

"Fine," she said, her breath hitching at his nearness. Oh, he smelled so good—like a forest just after a soft rain, like exotic spices mixing with warm butter, like...

She stopped thinking about Mick, determined to listen to the sermon. But somehow, now that they were all quiet and still, Mick managed to find her hand and hold it tightly to his. Somehow, she managed to steady her heart rate, sure that the entire congregation could hear it beating and flailing against the shiny cotton of her green-and-blue floral sheath. Somehow, a curling wisp of her long hair got caught against the crisp cotton of Mick's white button-up shirt, the curls holding to the fabric, pulling her to him each time either one of them took a breath. It seemed as if they were breathing in a rhythm meant only for them, a bit shaky, but steady and sure, measure for measure, as if their very breaths were dancing with each other.

Mick looked over at her and smiled.

Lorna knew she was in big trouble.

So she prayed while the preacher preached.

Dear Lord, what has come over me? Why am I acting as though I've never been around a man before? Why does Mick seem to affect me so strongly? I've never felt this way before, Lord. Remember Paris, when I thought I was so in love with Cole? And then he left, and now I don't think I even knew what love really was. Not even close. But my pride hurt all the same. Remember Italy, when I thought Dion was the only one for me? Can't even remember his face. Remember Ireland and Weylin? What was I thinking?

Didn't I learn anything from Cole's cruelty?

Oh, Lord, this is Mick, not Cole. This is the one who showed up when I asked you to send someone. I wanted someone strong, someone who could make me feel safe after the storm. And he does, Lord. He does. I'm so frightened, though. I can't let go. I'm afraid, Lord. So afraid. Help me to find peace. Help me to find the answers. Help me to feel safe in the dark, Lord. Show me what to do.

Lorna felt Mick's fingers tighten on hers, then she glanced down at his hand covering her own against the glowing brown wood of the pew. She chanced a look at his face, marveling in his little-boy features, marveling in the strength behind that innocent, lazy expression.

Mick's gaze found hers, held her there. Then he smiled and turned his attention back to the preacher.

Lorna went back to praying. She had to find some way of understanding the enormous emotions swirling like murky river water through her mind. She had to get a grip on the enticing, yet frightening feelings blossoming inside her each time she was with Mick. She couldn't rush this, couldn't give in completely. And yet, she felt as if she were falling down a dark, narrow tunnel. She had to shut her eyes to that particular fear. Mick wouldn't leave her stranded—not like the others. Not the way she always sabotaged herself and left herself stranded.

She'd been completely stranded and alone once. And since then, she'd never allowed anyone to get close enough to see the fear, the pain of that abandonment. How could she keep all of this from Mick? *How, Lord?*

Reverend Mahoney finished the sermon. "God is indeed our refuge and our strength. Even in times of trouble. Even when we don't see His hand reaching down to us. God was there with us during this terrible storm. Now it's up to us to rebuild and rededicate our lives to this town, and to His everlasting love."

Lorna wanted to feel God's hand reaching down to her, wanted to know God was with her, even in the dark. She knew inside her heart that she'd have to accept that, have to trust in God's guiding hand, before she could overcome her fears and make a firm commitment to any man.

She also knew that she wanted that man to be Mick Love. He hadn't let go of her hand—not once during the entire sermon.

He'd held on to her the whole time she'd been praying for God to send her a sign.

Chapter Eleven

❧

"Mick, thanks for stopping that near-disaster with the cypress tree the other day," Justin Hayes said, as they made their way through the covered dish buffet set out underneath the great oaks.

"No problem," Mick replied, his gaze zooming in on a large crispy chicken breast.

"You saved a cypress tree?" Lorna asked, curious. "What was the problem?"

Justin spoke up before Mick could. "Storm got it— you know that big one down by the water?"

"Of course," Lorna replied. "It's a favorite among the tourists. I didn't realize it'd been damaged."

"One of Mick's men found it and decided to just whack it up," Justin said, squinting as he spiked a drumstick and a sliver of honey-baked ham. "I was trying to stop him when Mick intervened and...settled things between us."

Lorna lifted a brow toward Mick, then studied Justin's face. Tall and lanky, he had reddish-blond hair and a temper to match. She wasn't surprised that he'd jumped on one of Mick's men for infringing on his territory. Justin protected the gardens like the keeper of the gate. And tried to protect Lacey in much the same way, in spite of her sister's gentle rebuttals and sometimes distant demeanor.

"We thought we were going to have to cut part of the main trunk down," Mick explained. "At least, David—our young and eager new team member—wanted to do that."

"Thing was split near in two at the top." Justin chewed a piping-hot yeast roll as he tried to talk. Waving a handful of roll in the air, he added, "That David boy was just about to take a chain saw to it—figured it would become an eyesore—right there at the water's edge, but Mick halted the young fellow just in time." He shot Mick an almost relieved look, then glanced around, no doubt searching for the trigger-happy David.

"David thought he was doing the right thing," Mick explained. "I'm just glad I found him in time to save the tree, and in time to save David from getting into a fistfight with Justin."

Justin didn't seem to mind any of that now, though, Lorna noticed. He just kept on talking.

"We reshaped it so that when it does grow back out, it'll probably be just fine. That tree's so old, but the roots and knees are intact and so peggy, it's almost completely hollow at the base. Time will tell about the top growing back in straight, though."

This time, he gave Mick a determined look, as if daring him to question this opinion. Then he marched away, obviously headed to find Lacey, his plate full of chicken, turnip greens, potato salad and rolls.

Lorna let out a hoot of laughter. "So you came up against the mighty Justin Hayes. Poor David. I'm so glad you came to that kid's rescue in time. I suppose no one bothered to tell sweet David that Justin rules the roost around here, as far as the landscaping goes. He's a royal pain, but very good at his work, and he's fiercely protective of these gardens."

"I don't blame him for that," Mick said, as they took their plates and headed for the summerhouse. "And I gave David a gentle but firm talking-to. He just got a little bit too ambitious. And as for Justin, I think he's tolerated *me* being here this past week because he knows I've got a hankering for the younger of the two lovely Dorsette women. Lacey is safe."

"But I'm not?" She grinned at him.

"A mighty strong hankering," he told her, his eyes holding hers.

A hankering? Was that what this was? She sure had a yearning inside her, too. But she kept that to herself as they strolled past where Lucas sweated and toiled, flushed and grinning, over a huge aluminum pot filled to the brim with steaming freshly boiled crawfish.

"Hey, Mick?" Lucas called, waving to them as he wiped his face and curling, humidity-soaked hair with the colorful bandanna he'd tied around his neck. "C'mon, man, and get some of these mudbugs while they're hot and spicy."

With that, he pulled on the handle of a large steaming colander full of spicy, bright-red crawfish, then dumped the whole thing unceremoniously across a long table covered with a white plastic cloth.

"Maybe later, friend," Mick called back, watching as people rushed to eat the mudbugs right off the pile in the middle of the table. "They do smell good, though."

Lucas winked and went right back to flirting with a leggy blonde who seemed extremely interested in getting a plateful of the little critters for herself.

"I see my brother has anxious customers lining up for his specialty," Lorna said on a droll note.

"And would that specialty be crawfish or that killer smile he's beaming out to all the single women here today?"

"You've figured him out, I see."

"It didn't take long. But I like your brother."

She only smiled and shook her head.

They stopped at the summerhouse. Mick glanced over at her and indicated a table just inside the cool shade of the open room.

Lorna wondered why they were automatically drawn to the rounded, octagon-shaped building, but at least today there were several other diners already there enjoying the breezes off the nearby bayou waters.

After they settled at a bistro table in a quiet corner, Mick straddled a chair, then glanced over at her. "Justin has every right to be protective, you know. This place is beautiful—that's why people come here. It's understandable that he wants everything to be perfect."

"So how did you manage to prevent him from throttling David?"

He took a bite of fluffy corn bread, closed his eyes in a moment of pure eating pleasure, then looked across the table at her. "First, I explained to David that the whole tree wasn't damaged. The tree was actually split about halfway up into two trunks—apparently happened when it was very young. David just thought the damage would eventually kill the whole tree, so he decided—without consulting anyone—to whack both trunks off about midway and leave it at that. But after I calmed Justin down, all we had to do was cut and shave the damaged trunk, then reshape the other trunk so it looked like a complete tree. I think with a little growth, it'll fill out just fine."

Lorna sat back on her chair, her food forgotten. "You've done it again."

"Done what?"

She watched as he sopped up turnip juice with his corn bread in typical Southern fashion. "Helped us out, saved us yet again. And this time, you saved poor shy David, too."

"David will toughen up eventually and...it was just a tree, Lorna."

"That tree has been at the edge of that swamp for well over one hundred-fifty years, Mick. It's more than just a tree. Don't you see, that's why we put up with Justin's temper around here. He loves each of these great oaks, and the magnolias and camellias and the cypress trees—they're like his children."

"He didn't have a problem about jumping on that boy, though."

"His temper will get the better of him one day, I'm afraid. I'm just sorry...and I apologize on his behalf. I'll be glad to talk to David, too."

"No, now, don't go and make matters worse by embarrassing David. He learned his lesson. And to his credit, Justin did apologize—grudgingly."

"That's good. And he should have, since you did save the tree in the end."

"Well, he was relieved when I came up with a solution. And just a tad irritated that he didn't figure out the process himself."

She gestured to indicate their surroundings. "There, you see. The trees, the grounds, the flowers—they're such an important part of this place. We're probably all a bit too protective—"

Mick grabbed her hand. "Lorna, I understand. Really, I do. Remember, I'm a tree person myself. That's why I wanted to save the cypress."

Groaning, Lorna sank back against her chair. "I'm sorry. You of all people, of course, understand."

"Tell me about the oaks," he said, his eyes bright with amusement. "That is, if you can keep calm while you're doing it."

"I'll try." She took a bite of fruit salad, sighed, then tried to relax. "A trapper planted them almost two hundred years ago. They were just saplings then, but somehow he must have known that they'd grow to be strong and tall one day. He planted them far enough apart that today they form that incredible canopy leading up to the house."

"Was the trapper your ancestor?"

"No. He moved on after selling the land to my family. The Dorsettes have lived on this bayou almost as long as those trees have been here."

Lorna saw the confusion mixed with regret in Mick's eyes.

"I've never had those kind of roots," he said, his voice low and edgy. "Seems as if I don't really have a family tree to call my own."

"Don't you have any relatives back in Mississippi?"

"None to brag about," he admitted. "My daddy's

family was always scattered and feuding. I've lost touch with all of them. My grandparents died when I was real young, so I never really had that kind of security. It was just my momma and me for a long time."

She nodded her understanding. "We lost both sets of our grandparents early. I have vague memories of my father's parents, but my mother's parents passed away before I was even born."

She waited for him to ask more about her parents, but he didn't.

"So Aunt Hilda's it for you?"

"She's it. And I do mean *it*. She has always been our link to the past and our link to our faith."

"What about your uncle, her husband?"

"He died of a heart attack years ago. But she never remarried. After our grandfather died, she just naturally took over this place and the town. She's been the mayor for close to twenty years."

"No one ever runs against her?"

"Why would anyone want to?"

"Good point."

They ate in silence for a while. Lorna listened to the laughter of the many children running through the gardens. She loved having people here again. Justin had done a wonderful job of replacing and pruning the damaged flowers and shrubs. And Mick and Josh had both pitched in way beyond the call of duty.

"When will you be leaving?" she asked now, her

gaze lifting to his, memories of their time here together so bright that she wanted to close her eyes.

Mick leaned forward, took her hand. "I guess we'll
be moving out, day after tomorrow. Claude had one
last trouble spot he wanted me to look at, then…"

He didn't finish the sentence. Lorna felt his eyes
move over her hair, her face, her lips. His eyes held
such a mystery, such a challenge.

"Where do we go from here, Lorna?"

"I don't know," she said, honest in spite of the
pain. "We always knew you'd have to leave. And
we're not kids on spring break. We're adults, Mick.
But I honestly don't know what's going to happen
with us now."

"Vicksburg isn't that far away."

"Might as well be a million miles," she stated, her
heart longing to find a spot on one of those utility
trucks of his and hang on for dear life.

"What does that mean?"

"It means that I can't leave Bayou le Jardin, and
you obviously can't stay. I have responsibilities here,
and you have to get back to your own work."

"Then we do have a problem."

"And no solution in sight."

"Not if you refuse to even consider just coming to
visit me."

"I can't, Mick. What would be the point?"

He reached across the table, touched her chin.
"The point is that I don't know how I'm supposed to

go on with life the way it was before I met you. The point is that I'm not nearly finished with you, Lorna. I want more. I want you to come and see me, to see how I live and work, to be sure."

"Sure of what? That I like being with you, that I'm attracted to you? I already know all of that, but it's useless to think we can keep this going."

"It's not useless," he replied, his anger snapping the words like twigs. "*We're* not useless. Something has happened here, Lorna, between us. You can't deny that."

"I'm not denying it," she said, her voice low and strained. "I'm just saying that I have to accept that you have a life back home that does not include me."

"But why can't it?"

She pulled away, threw up both hands. "Because when I came back here, I promised myself no more roaming, no more wandering. I'm secure here, I'm safe. I have a career I enjoy, and I have family around me. That's important to me, Mick. It wasn't before, but it is now."

"As it should be," he retorted. "But isn't having someone in your life, to share your life *with*, important, too?"

"Of course it is." She looked away, aware that the few other people in the room were watching them with curious expressions. "Let's drop this for now, all right? I don't want to spoil Aunt Hilda's celebration."

He got up, grabbed his empty plate. "Sure. I understand. I wouldn't do anything to upset your aunt. But this conversation is not over, Lorna."

With that, he stomped away, leaving Lorna to stare down into her own forgotten plate of food.

"But it is over, Mick," she whispered to herself. "I don't see any other way."

She wasn't ready to leave the sanctuary of this safe haven. Not even for the man with whom she'd fallen in love.

A couple of hours later, however, the decision was made for her. And for Mick.

Most of the churchgoers and townspeople had gone home to rest underneath fans and air conditioners that would hum them into a nice Sunday afternoon nap. The family and the Babineaux were busy cleaning away the trash and leftovers from the day's events, Mick included.

Josh came hurrying up the path from the guest cottages. "Hey, boss, we got trouble," he said, his breath huffing out with each word.

Mick turned from a nearby trash can. "What's up?"

"That storm that ripped through Shreveport and Monroe last night went straight for home, too," Josh told him, a cell phone in his hand. "A big pine fell right across one of the access roads into Battlefield Park. The power company cleared the road, but they want us to come on back to finish up the job. Seems there's several trees down around Vicksburg. We gotta get back.''

When Mick hesitated, looking at Lorna, Josh added, "Today, boss."

"I get it," Mick told Josh. "Do the other men know?"

"They're gathering their gear right now. Want me to call Claude?"

Mick nodded, looking down at the ground. "Yeah, tell him we can't finish that one spot we had pegged for tomorrow morning. And Josh, tell him we'll settle up the bill just as soon as I can process the paperwork. No hurry."

"Right." Josh pivoted to head back to the cottages.

Mick turned to find Lorna standing there with a stack of paper plates in her hands, her eyes on his face.

"You have to leave," she said evenly.

"Yes."

The word hung in the still, humid air between them.

"I don't have any other choice. They need us back home."

"Of course. I understand."

Mick wanted to grab her and make her admit that she didn't understand. How could she stand there, so cool and collected, her green eyes as unreadable as the murky waters of the swamp? How could she do that, when his heart was pounding and his head felt as if someone had hit him with a two-by-four?

"I thought we had more time," he finally said, turning to finish tying up the black trash bag.

When he turned back around, she was handing the plates to Rosie Lee. Then they were alone again. And yet she stayed silent and still.

"Well, say something," he finally said.

She shrugged, looked off into the bayou. "What's there to say? We knew this was coming. But I thought we had a couple more days, too. I guess it doesn't really matter, anyway."

Mick ran a hand through his hair in frustration. "It doesn't matter? Is that how you really feel? That we don't matter?"

She looked up at him, her eyes burning a bright angry green. "You have no idea how I feel, Mick."

"Oh, you're right about that. You don't want me to see how you really feel. And you'll just let me go, because you're too afraid to admit anything."

He saw that fear in her eyes, in the lifting of her chin, in the way her lips trembled in spite of her clenched jaw. He also saw a distant need in her eyes, the same need he felt in his heart.

So he reached for her—but she turned away.

"No, just go," she said in a whisper. "I told you there could be no 'us.' I told you we shouldn't get too involved."

"Yeah, well, I've never been good at listening to other people's advice."

Her head still down, she said, "Well, listen to me now. Just go back home, Mick. And forget about all of this. Forget about me. It's the best advice I can give you."

She started walking toward the house.

"Lorna—?" He took two long strides to catch up with her, and pulled her back around. "Don't walk away from me, Lorna. We can work this out."

She stared up at him, her eyes open and misty now. "How? Long distance? With me here, working at the restaurant, and you there, doing your own job? I don't want to leave this bayou, Mick. I can't."

"I wouldn't make you do that."

"Then I don't see how we can resolve this."

Needing to make her see reason, Mick took her hands in his. "Lorna, we found in one week what most people never have in a lifetime. I don't want to lose that."

But he could tell in her eyes, in her touch, that he already had. She went stiff in his arms.

"I've had other weeks, with other men, Mick. And they all managed to survive without me just fine. So will you."

That made him so mad, he could see little sparks of red rage flashing in front of his eyes. "And I guess you'll survive just fine without me, too, huh?"

"I've managed for this long," she said, her tone level and calm. "I'm really quite used to it."

He let her go, standing back to glare at her. "I never took you for a quitter, Lorna. Nor a liar. I guess I was wrong about us, after all."

With that, he turned and stalked toward the cottages.

Away from the harsh glare of her green eyes. Away from the resolved lift of her stubborn, trembling chin.

Away from the love he knew she felt inside her heart.

The same love he could never have denied her, the way she'd just denied him.

Chapter Twelve

The rain that the weatherman had predicted all week had finally arrived, and it seemed to be settling in for a good long stay.

Lorna stood at one of the large work tables in the restaurant, worrying over a *crème Chantilly* for tonight's dessert of *fraises des bois*—wild strawberries. She would delight her guests by telling them of the French custom of making a wish over the tiny delicate strawberries.

And maybe she'd make a few wishes of her own.

The *baron d'agneau Armenonville*—roast baron of lamb—was ready for tonight's crowd. The *canard à l'orange*—duck with orange sauce, served with wild rice and julienned vegetables, would be a hit, she was sure.

Everything was as it should be.

Except her broken heart.

She missed Mick with a knife-edged sharpness that cut into her very soul.

Had he really been gone a whole week?

It seemed like an eternity.

Lorna turned away from the rich fluffy cream. Hurrying to a huge wooden table in the middle of the restaurant's kitchen, she halfheartedly smiled at one of the Babineaux girls who worked with her and wanted to become a chef herself one day. Emily helped with the standard American and Cajun dishes. Right now, she had the beginnings of a rich, brown roux going for Lorna's famous Gumbo le Jardin—called that because most of the ingredients came right from the vegetable garden and swamp out back.

"You okay, Miss Lorna?" sixteen-year-old Emily asked as she stood beside Lorna and began helping her chop the onions, celery and bell peppers that formed the trinity of true Louisiana cooking. "Or are those onions getting to you?"

"It's not the onions," Lorna said, pushing with the back of her hand at the white chef hat planted atop her head.

"It's that man, then," Emily said with all the wisdom of a teenager, her thick Cajun accent becoming sharp with disapproval. "He ought not to have left you like that."

"I sent him away, Em," Lorna said, too tired and disillusioned to argue with the girl or deny the truth.

"You sure did," Lacey said from the doorway, an umbrella in one hand and a beige raincoat thrown over her shoulders.

Emily looked with wide-eyed fascination from one sister to the other, then quickly found work to occupy her across the long room.

"You're dripping water all over my floor," Lorna said to her sister with a sniff.

"Well, better get used to it," Lacey replied. "There's a flash flood warning out, and the forecast calls for even more rain. I don't think it's going to clear up anytime soon."

"Thanks for the update," Lorna retorted, angry at this intrusion. Her kitchen was her sanctuary, and she didn't need Lacey hovering over her like a mother hen, telling her she was making a huge mistake by letting Mick walk out of her life. "Now what do you really want?"

Lacey propped her umbrella out of the way against the wall, then shook out her raincoat before tossing it on a nearby chair. "I want to see my sister's pretty smile again. I want to laugh with you, talk with you. I want…"

She stopped, looked out the window where rain splattered on the green wrought-iron tables and chairs of the plant-filled courtyard.

"I want a lot of things," she finally said, coming to stand by Lorna.

"Well, we can't always get what we want," Lorna

snapped. Then because the onions *were* getting to her, she rushed to the sink to wash her hands and face.

Humiliated, she leaned over the running water, her shoulders shaking beneath her crisp white chef coat. Leave it to Lacey to make her feel even worse.

And leave it to Lacey to come rushing to her side to pull her into her arms. "Oh, honey, I'm so sorry. I didn't mean to upset you."

"It's not you," Lorna said into the floral print of her sister's flowing dress. She couldn't blame this discontent on her sister, and in spite of her harsh words, she was glad to have the shelter of Lacey's comforting arms. "I don't know, maybe it's the rain. I just miss him so much. Lacey, what's the matter with me? I've never missed anyone in such an awful way—not like this."

"You're in love," Lacey told her as she lifted Lorna's face and wiped at the tears trailing down her cheeks. "It's the best feeling in the world and also the most painful."

"Did you feel this way with Neil?"

"Every day of my life."

"Even now?"

"Even now."

Lorna pulled away, rubbing at her tears. "You see, that's why I can't do this. I can't love Mick. It just hurts too much."

"Only if you lose him—no, make that, only if you let him get away," Lacey pointed out. "But Lorna, you have to remember, like that old song says, it's better to have a little bit of love than to never know what love feels like at all.''

"Is that how you sleep at night?'' Lorna said, her words harsh again. "By telling yourself that you had one great love?''

The shock on Lacey's face made Lorna instantly regret that horrible remark. "Oh, Lacey, I'm so sorry. Please, just ignore me. Let me get through this in my own time and way. I'll be all right.''

But from the tormented look on Lacey's face, she wasn't finished with her little sister.

"You want to know how I go to sleep each night, Lorna? I curl up in that big bed and turn to the empty pillow at my side, and I remember...I remember the feel of Neil's hair underneath my fingertips. I remember the touch of his lips to mine. I remember the warmth of his arms, and the way he'd tell me he loved me as we drifted off to sleep.'' She stopped, took a breath, then held up a hand when Lorna tried to speak. "And it hurts. It hurts worse than anything you can imagine. But in spite of that awful pain, I always thank God for the time I had with Neil. I cherish those memories because they were the happiest times of my life. And I guard them, because I know I won't ever have that kind of love in my life again.''

"I'm sorry,'' Lorna said again, her eyes welling with fresh tears. "And I truly wish I could have what you and Neil had. You two loved each other so much, and I'm so sorry that you lost everything when he died. Honestly, I'd love to have some cherished memories of my own, even if it does scare me to pieces.''

"Then, do something about it. Go to Mick and tell him you love him. Work this out—whatever it takes—long distance or not. Don't punish yourself out of some sense of nobility or fear.''

Lorna headed back to the chopping table. "But he's there and I'm here, and…this just happened too fast. There's nothing to be done about it.''

"There's lots to be done,'' Lacey said as she walked toward the door. "Don't wait until it's too late.''

"Maybe it's already too late,'' Lorna replied.

"Just as water mirrors your face, your face mirrors your heart,'' Lacey said, paraphrasing Proverbs. "Stop denying it.''

Lorna watched as her sister silently left the room.

And outside, the rain came down in soft blue-gray sheets, the exact color of Mick's eyes the last time she'd seen him.

The rain hadn't let up for three days.

Mick stared out his kitchen window, down the bluff toward the dark, swirling Mississippi River below. And once again thought of Lorna.

Had this same rain washed over her? Had this same rain made her stop and think of him? Had this same rain made her feel gloomy and melancholy, edgy and full of discontent?

"Must be raining all over the world," he said aloud, turning to pour yet another cup of coffee. He'd learned how to make it strong now, just the way Lorna made it.

He looked down into the black brew, only to see his distorted reflection mirroring his innermost thoughts—and missed her all over again.

"I need to get back to work," he told the talking head on the blaring television set. "I need for this rain to go away."

But the weatherman on television was predicting even more rain all across the South. Leftovers from yet another big storm out in the Gulf. Mick was tired of fighting storms.

After taking care of the fallen trees he'd been called back to clear, he'd been shut up here for days, and he was running out of things to keep him occupied. He'd caught up on the mail, paid the bills, done all the necessary paperwork, talked to his accountants, harassed the bookkeepers, and growled and snarled whenever anyone called to check on him.

And to make matters worse, Josh had been going around grinning like an idiot because the man was so slap-happy in love with Kathryn that he couldn't contain himself.

Josh didn't mind telling Mick that he and Kathryn talked on the phone each night, and that he'd already made plans to go back to Bayou le Jardin come vacation time. Once Kathryn's cast was off, Josh and Kathryn planned to take a day-trip to New Orleans, to explore the sights and to continue getting to know each other.

"And after that, we'll see," his friend had said yesterday, that big grin conveying everything. "I think this is the one, Mick, my man."

"Sickening," Mick said now, as he slammed his empty coffee cup into the sink. He'd downed the coffee so fast, it had probably burned a hole right to his stomach.

That brought the question burning a hole through his heart right to the surface. Why couldn't he just pick up the phone and have a nice, normal conversation with the woman *he'd* left behind? Why couldn't he and Lorna have the same kind of happiness his friend and Kathryn were experiencing?

Mick looked at the phone, imagined picking it up, dialing the number for Bayou le Jardin, asking for Lorna. *Asking for Lorna.*

But, he reminded himself with a bitter groan, Lorna didn't want to be asked for, Lorna didn't want to take things any farther with him. She was afraid.

Did she think he'd hurt her, desert her?

Didn't she know him better than that?

The rain picked up, as if to answer his question with its constant pounding on his roof.

She *didn't* know him better than that. She didn't

know him at all. And right now, Mick couldn't blame her for sending him away. They'd had so little time together.

But that didn't mean a whole lot right now. He'd fallen in love, swiftly and surely. And he didn't know how to deal with that. And he certainly didn't know how to deal with her fears—of both the dark and him.

Maybe if he'd told her that he'd figured her out, that he'd seen her fear and wanted to help her get through it—maybe then, she would have trusted him. But he'd been a coward, afraid she'd turn away if he questioned her about her phobia. Mick had thought he could gain her trust by just being there with her. In the end, she'd simply given up and sent him away. She'd let him go without so much as a fight. And no faith in what might have been.

A commercial for a nearby church came on the television. Mick knew the church well. His mother had attended before her death, had insisted he attend with her at times, and Josh's whole family still went there.

Suddenly, it occurred to Mick that maybe Josh had something in his joyous smile, in his whole mind-set, that Mick had been missing. Josh had faith—in himself, in his budding relationship with Kathryn, and in God.

And in that instant, Mick realized he wanted that kind of faith. He needed it to make Lorna see that they could have a life together. He needed it to show her that she, too, had to have faith, that somehow God would see them through.

With a shaking hand, Mick turned off the television set and headed for the front door. He needed to talk to someone. He needed to turn back to God. Because in his own way, he was just as afraid as Lorna.

"Mick, I can't tell you how glad I am that you came by to see me today," Reverend Butler said as he got up to shake Mick's hand. "I hope I've helped answer some of your questions."

"You've helped a great deal," Mick replied, taking the older man's hand in his own. "I appreciate your taking the time to listen."

"That's part of my job," the reverend told him as he guided Mick out of his office. "You know you're welcome here anytime."

"Thanks," Mick said. Then he stopped and looked down the hall toward the sanctuary. "Would you mind if—"

"That's what it's there for," the reverend said, gesturing toward the sanctuary. "Go on in. God's been waiting for you."

Nodding, Mick slowly walked toward the darkened sanctuary. The rain was still falling, and the long silent room basked in shadows. But somehow, those shadows were comforting to him.

He entered, then stopped to look down toward the altar. His mother had forced him to come here. Had wanted him to have a church home in times of need, and in times of joy. But he'd turned away from all of that, simply because he'd blamed God for the sorry life his mother and he had had to endure.

This talk with God was long overdue.

"Hello, it's me," he said on a low whisper as he settled down on a pew in the middle of the high-ceilinged room. The pitter-patter of rain answered him as it hit the wide skylights over the altar. *"I know it's been a while. But I've talked to the preacher, and he says You don't mind that. Says You'll forgive me for staying away. He explained things to me. All this time I thought You deserted us, but You didn't. You gave my mother the strength to carry on, to become a self-sufficient person. You gave her courage, and for that, I thank You. I'm not so bitter about her death now. You took her home because she was a good and faithful servant, and she deserved some glory. The preacher explained that to me, too."*

He stopped, looked toward the skylights. Light seemed to be shining down on the altar, despite the rain and clouds. *"And I guess I have to forgive my old man, too. The preacher says I can't get on with my life until I let go of the bitterness toward my father. Will You help me let go of that, Lord? Will You teach me to forgive, to understand?"*

Mick listened to the rain, thinking it sounded very close to a melody.

"I need Your help here, Lord. I need to make

Lorna see that I won't desert her. She has such a sure faith in You, but she's afraid to let go and trust in me. Somewhere, somehow, she was hurt deeply, and now she's afraid of the darkness, afraid of being alone. Help me to show her that I won't leave her. And help me to see that You will never desert either of us.''

Mick stopped praying and sat for a while in the comforting enclosure of the church. He continued to listen. Really listen. There was a strange peace in just being still.

The rain kept on falling, like a great purge that at last released him from all the past hurts, from the yoke that he'd carried for so many years.

"I can make her a good husband, Lord. I have to believe that, before I can love her completely. I failed once. I didn't love Melinda enough to fight, because I think I was afraid that I'd fail—the way my daddy failed. I gave up, just like I gave up on You.'' He paused, took a deep breath, lifted his head to the sky-lights. *"I'm going to fight for Lorna. I need You on my side in that fight. And I promise, I will never give up on myself or You again.''*

Mick sat there for a few more minutes as the rain settled down to a gentle misting. A sense of complete peace came over him as he cast off all the guilt and pain of the past. He felt light, cleansed, content, at last.

He got up, then glanced back up at the skylight.

The rain had stopped, and for one brief moment, he thought he saw a ray of brilliant sunlight pushing through the dark clouds.

He smiled then, and knew the same joy that he'd always seen in his friend Josh's smile. Knew that at long last he, too, could find that certain joy.

He intended to share that joy with the woman he loved.

He intended to go back to Bayou le Jardin.

And this time, he wasn't leaving without Lorna.

Even if it meant he'd have to stay there for the rest of his life.

Chapter Thirteen

"**I**'m not gonna lie to you. It looks bad."

Claude Juneau sat across from Hilda Dorsette in the spacious parlor of Bayou le Jardin, surrounded by opulent antiques and freshly cut flowers. Lorna and Lacey stood behind their aunt.

It was Saturday, and because of that, Lorna and Lacey had convinced their aunt to stay home this morning. But already, Lorna could see the agitation and nervous energy radiating from her aunt's worried face.

"I can believe it," Lorna stated with a sigh. "For three weeks, either we've had to turn guests away or we've had them canceling out on us because of these spring storms. First the tornado, and now the possibility of flooding."

This turn of events didn't suit her already dark

mood, nor did it bode well for the already battered town or Bayou le Jardin's tourist traffic. Of course, knowing she couldn't control that only added to her dismal reckonings. Surely things would get better soon.

"How bad?" Hilda asked, a hand on Lorna's arm, no doubt to calm her niece as well as herself.

"Flash flooding of the roads," Claude said, shifting his big bulk as he tugged at his red suspenders. "More power outages from downed trees—their roots can't hold up in that soggy ground out there. I've got my men working, and, of course, we've got volunteers watching and waiting, too." He paused, then added, "And…we might have some problems with the levee."

"The river?" Lacey said, worry clouding her eyes. "We've never had trouble with the river—not too much, anyway. What are you saying, Claude?"

"I'm saying that we're gonna have to sandbag the levee. That water's rising mighty fast, and in some of them low spots, it's gonna spill over. I expect we'll see some homes and property get flooded. Which is why I came by. I wanted to warn y'all. This place might be knee-deep in water in a few hours."

"Bayou le Jardin?" Hilda asked, her eyes drawn to the ceiling-to-floor French windows that gave a clear view of the great oaks outside, and beyond that the levee. "The last time this place flooded was well over seventy years ago—the great flood of 1927."

Lorna looked outside, too. The flat, sloping yard was already standing in water. "Well, this could be the next great flood."

"That's what I'm telling y'all," Claude replied, a frown marring his ruddy complexion. "The city workers are up to their eyeballs trying to contain this thing, and the parish experts are predicting a big flood. Miss Hilda, we might have to call in the National Guard again. And we're gonna need everyone—every able body—to help with the sandbagging and the evacuation."

"If it comes to that," Hilda replied, her voice steady, her demeanor calm.

"It might," Claude said, standing to leave. "I knew you'd want the latest information so we could form a plan."

"Then, we'll be prepared," she told him, rising with the help of her cane and Lacey's arm on hers. "I'm going into town right away, to make sure everything's in place. Meantime, Claude, do whatever it takes to spare lives—that's foremost in my concerns. Then we'll worry about the property. I'll call City Hall right now and tell them the same thing."

"You'd certainly be safer there," Lacey told her.

"Lacey's right," the big man agreed. "You know I'll do whatever I can, and so will everyone else. But my advice to all of you is to get to higher ground before nightfall."

"Thank you, Claude," Lacey said as she escorted

him to the double doors at the back of the house, where he'd parked his truck in the driveway. "And please keep us posted until we can get there."

Lorna waited at the doors to the parlor for her sister. "What do you think? She's going to insist on going into town, but she's also worried about her home. Of course, she thinks this place is a fortress. And she certainly won't let us pamper her—not when she thinks others are in danger."

Lacey nodded, then whispered, "We'll just have to take matters into our own hands. We'll make sure she's safe." Then with a low rumble, she added, "Oh, it's just like Lucas to be off on some great adventure, when we need him here."

"Last I heard, he was headed out into the bayou. You realize we could get flooding from the swamp, too."

"Yes." Lacey nodded, frowning. "I just hope Lucas will have the good sense to come on home and help us persuade Aunt Hilda to leave before we get trapped in here."

"Children, come on back inside the parlor," Hilda called. "I'm not as deaf as you seem to think, and I don't cotton to whispering outside doorways when we've got so much work ahead of us."

Lorna walked back into the room. "We're just concerned, Aunt Hilda. We're thinking maybe you're smart to leave now—go on into town where it's safer."

Lacey nodded in agreement. "Or we could drive you up to Shreveport to see your friend, Cindy. You haven't had a good visit with her in such a long time, and you'd be safe up there."

Hilda stared at them through her bifocals, her lips pursed in a stubborn tilt. "Last I heard, it was raining upstate, too."

Lorna tried again, coming to stand by her aunt. "We just want you to be away from this mess. There's no need for you to be right in the thick of things."

"I'll go when I decide it's time," her aunt replied, her hand firm on the tip of her cane. But she turned to Lorna and placed her other hand gently underneath Lorna's chin. "And not one minute sooner." Then she dropped her hand and started out the parlor door. "I've got to find Tobbie and Rosie Lee. We've got to get busy salvaging what we can, in case the water makes it up to the house. I'll keep my phone near, so I can receive updates. But as soon as we have this place somewhat secure, I'm going to the office to oversee this problem."

Lorna gave her sister a knowing glance, then looked back out the wide windows. If they didn't make a decision soon, they might not have a minute to spare.

Checking the clock, Mick threw some clothes into his old, battered suitcase, then grabbed his cell phone.

Not wanting to waste precious minutes, he decided he'd call Josh from the road.

But he didn't have to make that call. The house phone rang even as he was heading for the back door. Debating whether to answer it, Mick looked at the caller identification number. It was Josh.

Mick picked up the phone. "Hello?"

"Boss, we got problems."

Groaning, Mick let out a sigh. "What now?"

"We gotta get back to Louisiana," Josh explained, his voice edged with worry. "They say there's been some major flooding around New Orleans and along the Mississippi, and they're expecting it to get even worse before nightfall."

Mick's heart stopped. "Bayou le Jardin?"

"Yeah, that's the word I'm getting," Josh said. "I...I have to go, Mick. Kathryn needs me—her momma won't be able to get all those children out in time if I don't go and help."

"I'm with you, man," Mick told his friend. "I'm on my way out the door right now. In fact, I was just about to call you to let you know I was headed back to see Lorna. But I didn't know there was a chance of flooding."

"C'mon by and get me," Josh said. "We'll have to drive it. The airports are booked solid, and every flight out is delayed because of this storm."

"We'll make it, Josh," Mick told him. "Just hold tight until I get there."

"Hurry," Josh said, before he hung up.

Mick did exactly that.

He had to get back to Lorna. He had to make sure her family was safe.

And he had to make sure that he told her how much he really loved her.

Lacey huddled with Lorna on the back gallery, watching as the rain continued to fall in angry, slashing sheets.

They'd worked steadily for the past couple of hours, securing the mansion as much as possible. Along with Tobbie, Rosie Lee and their daughter Emily, Lorna and Lacey had moved furniture and fixtures up to the second-floor landing.

But Rosie Lee was worried about her other children. "Little Tobbie is with his big brothers," she'd told Lorna, sounding worried. "I sure hope they're watching him."

"We'll get you home to them, I promise," Lorna had replied.

Because of Rosie Lee's worry, Lorna had paged Lucas to go and make sure the children were safe. When Lucas had come home, stating the family was fine for now, she'd sent him back out to take Tobbie and his wife home. There wasn't much else anyone could do now.

Aunt Hilda had pitched in, too, refusing to listen to her nieces' pleas. Even now, she was in her office, on the phone with a state trooper, getting the latest report on the flood conditions.

"I wish Lucas would come on back," Lorna said.

"Oh, I forgot to tell you," Lacey replied. "He insisted on taking Emily and Rosie Lee home himself, while Tobbie stayed behind to secure the outbuildings. He's probably holed up with the Babineaux clan, trying to keep them calm while they wait it out."

"Well, then, they might be in for a very long wait. Maybe he can convince them to get off that bayou while there's still time."

Lorna didn't think Lucas would be much help to them, anyway. The storm wasn't letting up. The restaurant was once again closed, the bed-and-breakfast shut down until the waters receded. She'd never seen her beloved gardens looking so lonely.

Which was exactly how she felt.

Preparing for the worse had taken her mind off Mick for a while, at least. But now as she stood here with her sister, wondering if they should stay or go, she longed for Mick to come around the corner in his hard hat with that wonderful grin on his face. She longed to hear his voice, reassuring her that everything would be all right.

But he's gone, she reminded herself. *You let him go. You told him not to come back.*

Shivering, Lorna placed her arms across her chest to ward off the wet chill. She couldn't think about

Mick now. She had to take care of her home and her family.

"We have to get Aunt Hilda out of here. She's champing at the bit to get into town. And if we don't do something soon, we're going to be trapped between the bayou and the river."

"Good thing Lucas has a boat."

"I'm serious, Lacey. Let's just go inside and tell her we've done everything we can here, and we'll take her to town."

"That means we have to leave, not knowing what will happen here."

"Well, what else can we do? I think everyone would be a lot calmer just having her there to lead them in prayer and keep them focused. And we do need to get her off this bayou."

Lacey gave her sister a long look. "Are you all right?"

Lorna knew what Lacey was thinking. "I'm okay with the rain, really. At least, there's no thunder and lightning."

"And no tornadoes this time."

"Just a lot of water." Lorna couldn't tell her sister about her intense loneliness. That would be admitting that she'd made a mistake in sending Mick away. Instead, she said, "So, do you want to tell Aunt Hilda we're ready, or shall I?"

Lacey thought about it, then nodded. "Why don't I talk to Claude first—see where things stand in town.

If they're already sandbagging, she'll want to be there. And she'll listen to Claude. That might get her mind off worrying about this place."

Lorna whirled around. "Okay, but why don't you drive her in—and to keep her from worrying about Bayou le Jardin, I'll stay behind with Tobbie and wait for Lucas. He should be home soon, and he can help me with any last minute problems."

"Did he take a cell phone or walkie-talkie with him?"

Lorna was already heading for the open hallway. "Who knows? I'll try to page him, but half the time he doesn't answer, anyway."

Lacey was right behind her. "Well, keep trying. Tobbie is down in the far gardens near the bayou, so he won't be much help—and you don't want to stay here by yourself, either."

Lorna hurried up the winding staircase, then turned at the curve. "I promise if I can't reach Lucas in an hour, I'll come on into town. We can spend the night in the school gym."

Lacey looked skeptical. "I'll find out from Claude if we can even make it into town."

"Okay. I'll meet you back down here."

Lorna rushed up the winding stairs and into her room, determined to page her brother. She tried Lucas's cell phone first, leaving a message for him to call her cell phone. Then she dialed his pager number and waited for him to respond.

Glancing around, she wondered what she should take if there was a flood. This bedroom was full of priceless artifacts and antiques. As was the whole house, for that matter.

"I can't let this storm destroy our home," she said, wishing Lucas would call.

The four-poster bed was bright and cheery, its comforter and pillows done in vivid shades of blue and yellow. She'd wanted it that way, to reflect the gardens outside. The pictures on the walls told the tale of her travels—some prints, some originals.

Monet. Picasso. Van Gogh. Wyeth.

Her vanity held exotic jars and bottles from various parts of the world. Her armoire held sundresses, and ball gowns, and faded blue jeans, and soft, worn sweaters and shirts. And hats—lots of hats.

"I need to wear my hats more often," she told herself, her nerves tearing at the calm she was trying so hard to hold on to. Crossing her arms in front of her, she stared at her reflection in the gilt-edged mirror over the vanity. "I need to do a lot of things."

Her cell phone rang, causing her to jump.

"Start talking, *belle,*" Lucas said, his voice coming in and out over a heavy static.

"Lucas, we need to get Aunt Hilda to town. The water is rising."

"Don't I know it. I'm down at the boathouse with Tobbie. They didn't come to sandbag?"

"Not yet. Aunt Hilda insisted that the main road

into town be taken care of first. All the houses
there—''

"I get it. Where are you now?''

"In my room.''

"How's the river?''

"It didn't look so good last time Lacey and I
checked. It's mighty close to coming over the levee.
What about you?''

"The bayou is full, sugar. Rosie Lee was frantic
about Tobbie being out here by himself, so I headed
out to look for him—ran into him in his pirogue. He's
checking the marsh, and I'm just helping him secure
a few things around the boathouse. Then he's gonna
go get his family, and we'll be outta here. You need
me home?''

"I need you home.''

"I'm on my way. Are you all right?''

"I will be when you get here. Lacey is going to
drive Aunt Hilda in. But I'll wait for you. Maybe
together, we can do something to hold back the water,
or at least move some more things to higher ground.''

"I'm coming, darlin'. You hang on.''

"Okay.''

Lorna hung up the phone, then hurried back downstairs. "I got in touch with Lucas," she told Lacey.
"He's down at the boathouse with Tobbie. But he'll
be here soon. What did Claude say?''

Lacey pulled her close. "He said to get her out of
here, and if that means bringing her to town to keep

her occupied, then so be it. And us, too. They've sandbagged the main area of town, but the road into Jardin is almost impassable.''

"Then take her. I told Lucas I'd wait here for him.''

"I won't leave you alone,'' Lacey replied. "Rosie Lee isn't here, remember? No one is here.''

Lorna put her hands on her sister's slender shoulders. "It's still light out. I'll be fine for another hour or so. Lucas is just down the bayou at the boathouse helping Tobbie. He'll be here in a few minutes, and in the meantime, I can move more things upstairs.''

"But—''

"You have to get Aunt Hilda to the shelter.''

"I don't like this. You don't have to prove anything to me, Lorna. Don't be foolish.''

This was an old argument. And one Lorna didn't have time for today. "I'm not trying to prove anything. I'm just worried about Aunt Hilda, and I won't leave without Lucas.''

Lorna watched her sister's concerned face, thinking she did need to prove something—to herself. It was time she quit depending on her family to hold her hand. It was time they learned that they could depend on her, too. She refused to remind herself that due to the years she'd tried to strike out on her own, she'd wound up coming home in a broken heap. She was tired of being broken. And she was tired of being afraid. Because of that, she'd lost Mick forever.

"I'll be all right, Lacey. Please don't worry. Lucas is on his way."

"I still don't like this."

Wanting to take Lacey's mind off *her* inadequacies, Lorna asked, "Is Aunt Hilda ready to go?"

"Yes, of course. She was ready two hours ago, but she knew we needed to do some things here, too. She's torn between staying to protect her home and going into town to protect the village." She paused, sighed. "I was very...elaborate with Claude's report. And I told her Lucas and you were taking care of things here, so that eased her mind some." She shrugged. "She thinks Lucas is close by."

"Well, he is, so get her in the truck and go. I promise I'll be fine. I'll get my flashlight and wait for Lucas."

She lifted a hand to wave away Lacey's still-obvious fears. "Look, it's midafternoon. And in spite of the rain, I have plenty of light yet."

"Oh, all right," Lacey said finally. "I can't fight both you *and* Aunt Hilda."

"I'll see you in a couple of hours," Lorna said.

A few minutes later, she watched at the back door as Lacey guided Aunt Hilda into the truck. Waving goodbye, she turned around, holding her flashlight securely close, just in case she needed it.

She'd make a strong pot of coffee and listen to the weather report, while she waited for Lucas. He'd probably be hungry. She'd make him a turkey sandwich. Then she'd start in the parlor, moving the rest of the odds and ends to the upstairs landing, at least. There was lots to do, lots to keep her busy.

Standing there alone in the kitchen, she said a prayer. *"Give me the strength, Lord. The strength I've been missing. I've been so afraid, of many things. I don't want to be afraid anymore."*

Everything would be okay. Lucas would soon be here to help her, and Lacey would take care of Aunt Hilda. They'd make it. They'd been through much worse, after all.

Except that Lorna had never before faced anything they'd been through completely on her own.

Chapter Fourteen

"**H**ow much farther?" Josh asked for the tenth time, as Mick's four-wheel drive truck zoomed down the interstate.

"An hour at most," Mick replied, watching the rain-slick roads while he pushed the gas pedal to the floor. "We'll make it, Josh. And when we get there, we'll probably find all of them safe and sound."

They'd tried calling every number they had between the two of them, but the phone lines were either messed up or completely down. They couldn't get through.

"Yeah, I know," Josh replied, leaning against the passenger door. "The Dorsettes can take care of each other. And they watch out for all the rest, too."

Mick had to smile at that. "Yeah, you know, I think that's what drew me to them. They are so tight-knit and close, but they don't exclude others because of that.''

Josh laughed. ''Nah, they just invite you right on in.''

They drove in silence for a few minutes, then Josh said, ''You're in love, too, aren't you, boss.''

Mick glanced over at his friend. ''Yeah, I'm afraid I am.''

''Nothing to be afraid of,'' Josh retorted, grinning. ''I knew it the minute I saw you and Lorna together. It just seemed...right.''

''Tell that to Lorna.''

''No, man. You gotta be the one to do the telling.''

Mick nodded. ''That's why I'm headed down the interstate, friend.'' Then he reached over to punch Josh's muscular forearm. ''And what about you? When did you know it was 'right' between Kathryn and you?''

Josh chuckled. ''The minute I went down into that crumpled building to find her. Or I should say, the minute I laid eyes on her.''

''But it was dark down there,'' Mick pointed out. ''How could you fall in love with her without even seeing her?''

Josh touched a big hand to his heart. ''I saw her inside here, man. I saw her heart, her soul. That woman has spunk. I felt her strength.'' He shook his head, his tone full of awe. ''Even trapped in a collapsed building, with a broken leg, she still had more courage than I'll ever have. I didn't need a spotlight to show me what Kathryn's all about.''

Mick couldn't respond to that. He didn't have the words for a snappy comeback. But he did know what Josh was saying. ''I guess that's why I love Lorna,'' he said at last. ''I saw her courage that day when I pushed her away from that falling limb.'' He smiled again. ''I saw so much in her eyes—bravery and defiance—but I guess what really caught me was her wariness.''

Josh lifted two dark brows. ''Wariness? That's a new one. Most women aren't in the least wary when it comes to being around Mick Love.''

''Exactly,'' Mick replied with a wry grin. ''Lorna didn't fall for my earth-shattering good looks and glowing smile.''

Josh sat up, laughing. ''Get outta here. She fell all right, and fell hard.''

''But she had my number.'' Mick tried to explain. ''She didn't want to rush into anything.''

''And that's how you two left it—just hanging out there? Y'all couldn't reach a compromise, at least?''

''Lorna doesn't want a compromise. That wariness has her running scared.'' He shrugged. ''And she won't tell me what she's really afraid of, even though I think I have that figured out. It's complicated. *She's* complicated.''

''So…she loves you, though, right?''

"I think she does. At least, I intend to find out if she does."

Josh shook his head. "Sounds like you're gonna be bailing a big bucket of water in this flood, my friend."

"Let's hope I don't wind up drowning in regret," Mick replied.

They both groaned at their attempt at symbolism.

"Let's just get there and make sure they're all safe," Josh said, his tone serious. "Then we'll worry about all the rest."

Mick nodded in agreement. "A few more minutes. We'll be at Bayou le Jardin before nightfall."

Lorna glanced out the back door again. It would be nightfall in about an hour. And Lucas wasn't home yet.

"Lucas, where are you?" she asked as she tried his phone again, irritation covering the shiver of fear running through her voice.

She moved away from the window, then looked around the kitchen. She'd done what she could to prepare the room. All the food was up on the counters and in the higher cabinets. She'd moved pots and pans into the big pantry.

The place looked as if she were getting ready to move permanently.

After organizing the kitchen, she'd gone through the downstairs rooms, removing antique knickknacks and priceless artifacts, taking them one by one upstairs to the highest level of the house. All the upstairs bedrooms now were full of portraits, porcelain figurines, valuable vases, rococo candlesticks, and what few Chippendale dining chairs she'd managed to lug up the winding stairs. There was little else she could do on her own.

So she walked the long central hallway, checking yet again for anything that might be damaged if the water kept rising. She knew the heavy Hepplewhite secretary in the hallway would be ruined—

"Stop thinking about that," Lorna said aloud, her voice echoing eerily down the empty hallway. "These are just things. Just things." And yet, she knew she'd fight the flood to keep these precious "things" intact. They were part of her heritage, after all.

Maybe that explained the sense of calm falling over her. That, and her thoughts of Mick. Whenever she felt the fear creeping in like a wave of relentless water, she remembered how safe she'd felt with Mick out on the levee. She thought about his touch, his kisses, the security that being in his arms had given her.

"We had so little time together," she whispered. Yet, somehow, her time with Mick had begun a healing process inside her. She would be all right. She would survive this, just as she'd survived so many crises in her life. If nothing else, she had Mick to thank for that.

Her cell phone rang, the singsong noise snatching her back from her thoughts. "Hello?"

"*Chère,* we've got problems."

"Lucas, where are you? What's happened?"

"Tobbie got a call from home. One of the children—" Static cut him off.

"What? I can't hear you, Lucas."

"...missing."

Lorna heard that one word loud and clear.

"...got to help them...looking for the baby—Tobias. He ran off—said he was going to climb high up in a tree."

"Go, go!" she shouted into the phone. "Lucas, don't worry about me. Find him, find Tobias."

Lucas said something else, but she couldn't make it out. Then the phone went dead.

Little Tobbie—out there alone in the rain.

Little Tobbie was only eight years old, the baby of the Babineaux clan. Lucas had to find him. Lucas *would* find him. After all, *he* knew what it felt like to be alone in the rain and dark.

With water everywhere.

And so did she.

Lorna looked out onto the back gallery. Already the flat green stone was covered with about six inches of water. Already that same water was slowly rising up the couple of inches to the door frame.

The flood was coming.

She was still very much alone.

And darkness was beginning to fall.

Lorna automatically headed back into the kitchen to find her flashlight. Then she went around flipping on lights and turning on lamps. Lucas wouldn't be here for a long, long time. She'd have to leave without him, hoping that he found Little Tobbie, hoping that they'd all be safe.

She decided to go to the upstairs gallery facing the river to see how well the levee was holding. Then she'd come around to the other side, toward the back gardens and the bayou. Maybe she'd be able to see how high the water was from there.

If not, she'd have to go ahead and drive out on her own. Her little second-hand sportscar wouldn't be too safe in a raging flood, but that was her only choice.

Lorna stopped on the second-floor landing, surveying the scattered possessions she'd hurriedly assembled there earlier. Among them was the portrait of her parents that had been hanging in the downstairs parlor. She wouldn't let the flood waters damage that. She would carry it out of here on her back, if she had to.

Pushing back memories of another night and another raging storm, Lorna moved toward the French doors to the gallery, then opened them to stand on the porch.

The rain kept falling, softly now, but with a cadence that had an almost soothing quality. She looked through the dusky, gray light to the river.

And her heart stopped.

The water was beginning to tip the levee. She could see it gleaming blue-black against the approaching night. The saplings and reeds nestled on the other side of the levee were now under a murky wall of water.

Panic seizing her body, she spun around to head up the hallway toward the back of the house. She wanted to see the bayou, to find her brother.

What she saw there terrified her even more.

More water. It was hard in the dim to distinguish where the bayou left off and the yard began. The restaurant was slowly becoming submerged. She was glad that she and Lacey had earlier tried to secure some of its furnishings and supplies; she could see the water lapping hungrily at the seats of the wrought-iron chairs on the low back patio. In another few minutes, the water would be inside her beloved restaurant kitchen.

And there was absolutely nothing she could do about it.

"Stay calm, Lorna," she told herself. Reaching for her cell phone nestled in the pocket of her baggy walking shorts, she dialed Lucas's number again. And got no response.

Then she tried Lacey. Her sister answered on the second ring.

Through the static, Lacey asked, "Lorna, where…you? I thought you and Lucas…behind us."

"I'm still waiting for him, but I don't think he's

coming anytime soon. Lacey, he hasn't made it in from the swamp. Tobias is missing. Lucas had to go look for him.''

"Oh, no. Oh…Little Tobbie?"

She heard the panic in her sister's voice, felt that same panic lifting like a fierce, fast-moving wind over her body.

"Listen to me, Lorna. Just get…car and come into town. You've still got time. The sandbags are holding so far…road…passable. But…different story in a few hours. Just come on, honey."

"I can't leave without Lucas—he's got to find that child. I can't leave until I know they're both safe."

"Yes, you can." Impatiently, Lacey snapped, "Why did you have to pick a flood to try and prove your courage?"

Tears sprang to Lorna's eyes. Tears of longing, tears of regret. "I don't know. I guess because of Mick."

"Mick? What's he got to do with this?"

"I…I wouldn't give him a chance, because I was afraid…afraid he'd leave me. You know I always have to be the first one to leave, right?"

"Yes, I know that. But…you're still smarting from being jilted by Cole. I don't think Mick is anything like Cole Watson."

"But what if he can't deal with me?" Lorna asked, her eyes watching the water. "What if he can't understand my…fear?"

"Can't we talk about this later?" Lacey said gently. "Just come into town, Lorna. Now."

"Okay. I'm coming," Lorna finally said. "But I'm so worried about Lucas."

"Lucas knows that swamp like the back of his hand," Lacey reminded her. "I'm sure he's going to find Little Tobbie safe and sound. But *you* can't wait. We'll just have to send some of the men out to find all of them. And you, too, if you don't hurry."

"What if…" Lorna couldn't finish the thought.

"He'll be fine," Lacey replied, but the words sounded hollow and dull. "Now, come on, before we have to send someone to rescue you."

Lorna hung up the phone and looked out toward the trees.

No sign of Lucas.

She turned back inside. She'd just grab her raincoat and go. Her hands shaking, she found her car keys and donned a long beige trench coat. Sending up prayers for her brother, for her family, she started down the stairs, her flashlight in her hand even though lights were blazing throughout the house. At the bottom, she stopped.

"My parents' portrait." She ran back up the stairs to grab the rectangular picture, its gold-etched frame shining like fire in the lights from the chandelier over her head.

Glancing around one last time, she turned to rush back down the stairs.

And that's when the lights went out.

* * *

Mick pulled the truck up to the town square in Jardin, then turned off the motor. He was dog-tired and worried, but at least he was here now. He'd find Lorna, and everything would be all right between them.

"Looks like the town's safe so far," Josh said as he rounded the truck, stretching his sore body in the process.

"Let's go find them."

They headed to the mayor's office. And came face to face with Laccy.

Mick took one look at her and knew something wasn't right.

"Mick," she said, grabbing his arms with white-knuckled fingers. "I'm so very glad to see you. And you, too, Josh." She touched Josh's arm. "Kathryn is in the back conference room with Aunt Hilda. She's safe, but they're still trying to round up her family."

Josh nodded and took off down the hallway.

That left Lacey staring up at Mick, a fear brightening her blue eyes.

"What is it?" Mick asked, scanning the hallway behind her. "Where's Lorna?"

Lacey lowered her head. "She's at the house. She was waiting for Lucas to come in from the bayou."

Mick swallowed the lump of cold dread that had formed in his throat. "And?"

Lacey looked up then, and he saw that same dread

on her face. "Lucas never made it home—Little Tobbie is missing, and Lucas had to go back out and help search the bayou…to find him. Lorna is still there, alone. She was supposed to be on her way here, but that was over an hour ago. And we just got word that the power's out in some parts of the parish."

"What?" He pushed Lacey away, then dropped his hands to his side. "You left her there alone, knowing…knowing how things are with her?"

Lacey gasped, her hand coming up to her mouth. "You mean, *you* know?"

"That she's afraid of the dark?" He nodded. "It didn't take a whole lot to figure it out." Then he whirled around and headed to the door. "I have to get to her. She must be terrified. Why did you leave her like that?"

Lacey blinked back tears. "I didn't want to. But Lorna insisted that Lucas was on the way, and we had to get Aunt Hilda to safety. Oh, Mick, I'm so sorry. You have to get her."

Mick didn't bother answering. He only knew that his heart felt like a lead weight bobbing against his chest. He only knew that the courage he'd seen in Lorna's eyes the first time he'd met her had been a big front.

He had to reach her.

He went back out into the darkness and got into

his truck. Water rushed all around the vehicle as he backed it out into the street.

"Lord, I need You now. Lorna needs You. Help her to hang on until I can get there, Lord. Help all of us."

Chapter Fifteen

Mick made it to within sight of the house. Just as he rounded the curve leading to the gate, the road became impassable. There was a low spot in the levee, and through the beam of his truck's headlights he could see the river water rushing over the spot in swirling urgency.

He got out of the truck, stared down into the water, and decided it was too risky to try to drive through it. If he got stuck—or worse, carried off on the river currents—that wouldn't help Lorna.

He'd have to go the rest of the way on foot. Which meant he'd be tracking through knee-high water.

Quickly, he went back to the truck and managed to pull it over to the side of the road, up onto the levee. Then he got a flashlight and a first-aid kit out of the big toolbox on the back of the truck. He didn't want to think about having to use the kit.

After securing the truck, he started trudging through the water, his hard hat and yellow slicker his only protection against the pounding rain. Once he was away from the beam of light the truck had provided, he realized just how dark it had become. Lorna would be terrified if she was alone in this blackness.

Then he saw the silhouette of the big house up ahead. It was completely dark, too.

Mick ran the rest of the distance to the front gate, and with shaking hands managed to get it open despite the rushing water pushing it back. Then he was in the front gardens, underneath the cloying dark canopy of the great oaks.

"Hang on, baby," he said into the wind and water washing over his face. "I'm coming."

He followed the bouncing beam of his powerful flashlight, hoping Lorna would at least see it and come out to find him. But as he got closer to the house, a solid wall of fear slammed into him.

The entire bottom floor of the mansion was covered in at least six inches of water.

Mick sloshed through the water, his jeans now completely soaked. "Lorna?" He shouted her name above the din of rain and wind. "Lorna, it's Mick. Can you hear me? Lorna, are you in there?"

Figuring she probably couldn't hear him, anyway, he tried the front door. It was locked. Mick hurried around the first-floor gallery, his heavy work boots pushing at the dark water. He reached the kitchen, then tugged at the French doors. They opened with a groan against the surging waters.

"Lorna?" He beamed his flashlight over the room but didn't see anyone. He did see, however, that Lorna had managed to stay busy. Everything was up high, away from the floor. She'd even turned the high-backed chairs up onto the long, butcher-block table.

He moved toward the central hallway, his wet clothes and shoes hindering each step as he pressed against the current of the flowing water. "Lorna?"

The flashlight's single beam showed someone had worked hard here, too. The hallway was practically stripped: no rugs, no potted plants, no artifacts. Whoever had moved things had only left the things that couldn't be lifted.

He came to the front parlor and searched across the hall in the formal dining room, doing a quick once-over with the flashlight. Again, the rooms looked as though someone had robbed the place, with portraits and paintings missing, and all the furnishings stripped of their ornaments and decorations—even the chairs turned up on top of the table.

He quickly turned from the dining room to the parlor. Most of the furnishings here were bare, too. And the portrait of Lorna's parents was gone from its place of honor over the fireplace.

"Lorna," he said, whispering to himself now. "Where are you? Why did you pick today to stay here on your own?"

Mick supposed her fear had driven her to stay busy. His heart ached to comfort her, to hold her and tell her she was safe now. But first, he had to find her.

He started up the stairs.

Glad to be away from the water's strengthening current below, he stopped on the third stair to move his light up to the landing, hoping to find her there. Instead, he found most of the missing things from downstairs.

Shaking his head, Mick put down the first-aid kit, then took off his heavy, dripping wet slicker. He slowly made his way around the winding staircase. "Lorna? Honey, are you up here? Where are you?"

No answer.

She had to be somewhere upstairs. It was the safest, most logical place to get away from the rising waters. But then, in her state of mind she might not be thinking logically.

"Lorna? he called, sharper this time. "It's Mick. I'm here, Lorna. I'm here."

They were coming for her. She had to hide, had to stay still, just as Lucas had warned her to do. She had to find Lacey. Lacey would hug her close and keep her safe. Lacey on one side and Lucas on the other, here away from the rain and the storm, away from the water and the darkness. That's the way it had always been.

Away from those horrible, bad men who'd killed their parents.

"Just stay still and quiet," she told herself. The same words Lucas had repeated to her over and over again as they'd hidden there in the darkness, his hand sometimes clamping down on her mouth to keep her from screaming or moving.

If I move, they'll find me.

She didn't dare breathe, didn't dare call out. The darkness moved over her like a hot, wool blanket, thick and suffocating. But if she tried to push at it, tried to breathe, they would find her and kill her, the same way they'd killed Mommy and Daddy.

Where was Lucas? Where was Lacey? Why had they left her here all alone? Weren't they supposed to be here, too? They'd always, always been here with her. She remembered them being here, could almost feel them on each side of her, protecting her.

That's the way it had been.

But then she remembered how she'd tried to outrun the fear. How she'd left her family behind to strike out on her own. And for a while, it had worked. She'd taken off to Europe, always running, trying to escape the great fear that chased through her dreams and taunted her even in her waking hours.

But, that had to be it—she must be dreaming again.

That was why Lucas and Lacey weren't here. They would never leave her alone in the dark. Never.

Yes, that was it. She was having that same horrifying, familiar nightmare. The one she'd fought against for so very long. The one she'd paid countless therapists to help her cure. And for a while, it had been dormant. Until the tornado had brought it all crashing back.

Tired. She was so tired. But she couldn't sleep. The men might find her and kill her. She had to stay awake, had to stay calm.

The darkness trapped her. She couldn't move. She could hear the rain falling, falling, never stopping. She could almost reach out and touch the water creeping ever closer to her hiding place, here underneath the house on the hill.

But she wasn't underneath the house on the hill, she reminded herself. For a brief instant, that gave her a measure of calm and relief. She was at Bayou le Jardin. Safe. She'd always been safe here. God had watched over her here. Was He watching over her now?

Lorna tried to focus, tried to remember what had happened to her flashlight. Had she dropped it, or had the batteries burned out? *Can't remember. Must not remember.*

She held the memories at bay, along with the fear. She pushed at the horrible, clinging fear, fought it, refused to acknowledge it.

But she could hear *them* coming. She could hear
the footsteps, the movement of man against water, the
ripple of waves as the dark water lapped ever closer
to her hiding place here amid the tangled vines and
undergrowth behind the house on the hill.

You're not there, she silently shouted to herself.
*Lorna, get a grip. You're at Bayou le Jardin. Don't
panic.*

But she'd already reached that point.

She tried to speak. "Lucas?" But the word, his
name, had no sound. "Lacey?" Why wouldn't her
throat cooperate?

The footsteps were getting closer now.

Her heart was beating so loud, so fast, she knew it
would give her away. It sounded so much like the
beating of the drums.

This time, they'd find her.

But this wasn't how it was supposed to end. Lucas
and Lacey were supposed to be here with her, and
they'd stay here just like this until morning, when the
authorities would come and get them.

And then, they'd be sent home to Aunt Hilda.

And Mommy and Daddy would be sent home, too.
In their coffins. They would be buried by the Chapel
in the Garden.

Home.

But she *was* home. She was safe. Why was it so
dark? Where was everyone?

Lorna shook her head, tried to focus in the darkness, tried to find air. Somewhere in the center of her being, she felt a core of steel giving her the strength to hang on. And somewhere, deep in her soul, she heard a voice.

Be still, child. You will survive. Trust in the Lord with all of your heart.

Then she heard the footsteps again. With a gasp, she realized they were near—right outside her hiding place.

They'd found her. The bad men had found her.

And she was all alone.

Then all the memories came rushing toward her like the great raging river bursting through the levee. And she knew this was no dream. This was real, and she was once again alone in the dark.

Giving in to sheer terror, Lorna opened her mouth and screamed. The fear that had chased her for so long had become a real and tangible thing, gripping her like a twisting vine as she thrashed against the cloying black night.

Mick heard the scream.

It was a sound he would never forget.

He shouted her name. "Lorna!"

He was just outside the door to her bedroom. Not bothering to stop and think, he kicked with his boot at the locked door, shattering the frame, sending wood flying out before him.

"Lorna?" He called her name over the scream,

then sent the beam of his flashlight around the big square room.

No sight of her. Yet the scream was echoing all around him.

Taking a breath to regain control, Mick stood still. Then he put the flashlight on a nearby table, and waited until the screams subsided.

The silence was just as loud. It was filled with her fear.

Dear God, what caused her to come to this?

Mick understood so much now. He understood why Lorna had run away from every relationship she'd ever had. And he certainly understood why she'd pushed him away.

But he had to show her that he wasn't like the others. He wouldn't leave her again. Ever. He waited in the silence, a cold, shivering sweat mixing with the rainwater covering his body. And he listened.

God, help me. Guide me to her.

He heard a sniff, a sob, and then he heard her labored breathing, as if she couldn't get enough air.

"Lorna?" He said her name softly this time, then he moved a step closer to the sound of the sobs.

She was in the closet.

Mick heard the shuffling of her body. She was trying to move away. "Lorna, listen to me," he said, his voice firm in spite of his shaking insides. "Lorna, it's Mick. Honey, it's all right. Do you understand?

I've come to help you. I'm going to get you out of here, okay?''

Mick listened again, straining to hear over the sound of rainfall.

He didn't know how to help her. He'd never encountered this kind of deep-seated terror. So he prayed, silently and with total dependence on God to guide him.

And then he started talking.

"Lorna, remember our nights out in the summerhouse? Did you feel safe with me there?" When she didn't answer, he continued, his voice soft and soothing. "You must have. You stayed there with me long after the moon had come up. Think about that, honey. Think about how we laughed and talked and cuddled. Remember? I held you in my arms, and we listened to the frogs croaking out in the bayou. We listened to the crickets singing and those pesky mosquitoes humming around our ears. Lorna, that was magic for me. You brought me such a sense of peace, such a sense of belonging. You taught me how to have faith again.''

He stopped, waited. Prayed.

"Lorna, you can trust me. You can tell me anything. I'm not going to judge you or condemn you. I understand everything now. I know what you've been fighting against.''

Again he stopped. Hoped. Listened.

And all the while, he knew the water was rising.

He had to get her out of here.

So he tried one more time, based on a hunch and sheer desperation. "Do you want to tell me about that night? The night your parents died?"

He thought he heard a sob. He stopped breathing just to hear it again.

And then he heard her voice.

"They…they came to our camp in the middle of the night."

She sounded so small, so lost, that it took every ounce of strength he had left to keep from rushing into the closet to pull her close.

But he held back. "Who came to your camp?"

"The rebels," she said, her voice growing stronger. "They didn't like us being there. They…didn't want missionaries in their village."

Missionaries. Mick swallowed that bit of information right along with the knot in his throat.

"Where was your camp, Lorna?"

"Africa," she said. She was silent for a minute. "Somewhere far away—a very remote spot in Africa. Mommy and Daddy wanted to help…they wanted to take care of people. God sent them there, you know."

He heard another sob. Pushed at the tears burning his own eyes. "But the rebels…they hurt your mommy and daddy?"

"They murdered them," she said at last.

Then Mick heard the sobs coming as softly and surely as the rain falling outside the open French doors. And he wondered if she'd ever allowed herself to cry like this before.

"And what about you? How did you get away?"

"We hid. Lacey and Lucas pulled me out of my bed and we ran and ran. Daddy told them—get away—run—run."

Mick swallowed again, closed his eyes to the horror she must have suffered. They'd all suffered.

"Where did you hide?"

"Underneath the house on the hill. The hut. It was round and open." She stopped. Took a shuddering breath. "Like the summerhouse, only it was dark and...it was up on stilts. There were snakes underneath there—and spiders, big spiders. But the storm was coming. Rain. So much rain. And wind. A big storm. And the men who'd hurt my parents were still in our compound."

She was talking now, her voice growing stronger with each word, sounding more like herself. Mick didn't interrupt. He knew deep within his soul that she needed to tell this story.

"But Lucas held my mouth shut so I wouldn't scream, and he pushed me under there. Lacey came in with me. She held me in her lap and rocked me. She was crying. Then Lucas came in and pulled the vines back around us. So many vines. They held me there, in the dark. We waited. We heard the men roaming around, walking past us, running in the rain and mud. They came up inside the round house, above our heads. We heard them talking as they searched.''

She stopped, sighed.

Mick stepped toward the closed door separating them. "What happened then?"

"The storm," she said, her voice edged with fatigue.

"The storm was getting worse. Flooding. Water. We were safe up on the hill. Dry behind the vines. But the water was coming, so they...they finally left."

Mick didn't ask what happened next. Instead, he held his breath. Hoping she'd keep talking.

She did. "We stayed there until morning. The rain finally stopped and daylight came. Then Lucas told Lacey and me to stay put. He was going out to find help. We didn't want him to go out there, but Lucas told us to be still. Then he left us there."

"Was he able to find someone?"

"Yes, he ran to a nearby village. A friendly village. Then the authorities came and...told us our parents were gone...dead. But we knew that already." She paused again, then said, "We stayed at another compound for a few days, and then we came to live with Aunt Hilda."

Mick took off his forgotten hard hat and ran a hand over his hair. He couldn't imagine the terror the sisters and their brother must have suffered that night. Alone in the dark, in a remote jungle, caught in the middle of a raging storm, with rebels and poisonous creatures lurking about. Alone for hours on end. They must have thought everyone had abandoned them.

Even their God.

But then Mick realized something that the three never had. *The storm had saved them.* It had caused the rebels to flee.

He wiped away tears that he hadn't even known were falling. No wonder this incredible woman was so afraid of the dark. And no wonder her family had protected her. Lacey and Lucas had taken care of their little sister on that horrible night, and they were still trying to take care of the woman she'd become. In her own way, Lorna had rebelled against all of it—running away across the world to prove she could do things her way. Only to return home to the sanctuary of her family and Bayou le Jardin.

Mick wanted her to find comfort and sanctuary in his arms. He'd make her see that she could trust him. And he'd make her see, just as he'd had to see, that God had not abandoned her.

"Lorna, listen to me, okay?"

"Okay," she said on a whisper. "Mick?"

The hope in her voice, in the way she said his name, made him want to cry all over again. He shut his eyes to the tears. She knew who he was, at least.

"It's me, honey. I'm here and I'm not going to leave you. Can you see the light? Can you see my flashlight?"

"Yes. Mine…quit on me. I…lost it, and I got scared. I wanted to show them I could do this—but I guess I'm still scared, after all."

In spite of her confession, she sounded stronger now, more coherent.

"It's all right to be scared, Lorna. I was scared myself. Scared of loving you, scared of giving up my pride. I was scared of turning back to God, of giving Him control."

"Really?"

"Really. But I had a long talk with my pastor, and then I had a long talk with God. I'm not scared anymore."

"Is that why you came back here?"

"I came back for you," he told her, his voice low but clear. "I had to see you again. I had to be here with you."

"God sent you." The statement was both solemn and full of awe.

"Maybe He did," Mick replied, closing his eyes in thankfulness. "I'm here now, honey, and I'm not going anywhere."

She was silent for a minute, then she said, "Even though I'm a coward?"

"You are no coward, Lorna Dorsette. You are one of the bravest women I've ever known. Now, stop this foolishness and come on out here so I can hold you in my arms."

She became silent again. Mick felt the tension in his neck, twisting him like a vice. "Lorna, please."

"I'm not...sure. I'm still...afraid."

"Lorna, you don't have to be afraid anymore. You know why?"

"Why?"

He sighed, fell to his knees right by the closed door.

"I think I've figured this out, baby. Even though the rebels killed your parents, God didn't abandon you that night. Do you hear me?"

"I hear you."

He took another breath, closed his eyes. "The rain came, remember? That raging storm saved you and Lacey and Lucas. Those men went away because of the water. It scared them away."

Silence.

Mick breathed, knowing that they were breathing together—a slow, steady rhythm of hope in the midst of so much darkness.

"I never thought of it like that," she said at last. And then she added, "Why didn't the rain come sooner? Why didn't God send it to save my parents?"

He surely didn't have an answer for that one. Except the one the preacher had given him. "Maybe God had a different plan for them. Maybe they had to die in order for you to have a different life. God needed them in heaven, Lorna."

Then he heard the anger.

"Yes, and He took them and left us all alone."

Mick edged closer to the door, touched the knob. "No, Lorna. It's horrible that your parents had to die, but God didn't desert you that night."

"I don't believe you."

Slowly, Mick turned the knob. "Lorna, listen to me. I'm going to open this door so you can see the light."

"No!"

He stopped, then tried again. "Yes, I'm going to come in there and get you. And I promise you, I will never leave you again. And neither will God."

"How can I be sure? Cole left me standing at the altar. He was afraid of living with me. He thought I was crazy."

Surprised, Mick asked, "Now why would he think that?"

"The nightmares," she explained. "The horrible dreams. He laughed at me when I told him. Laughed at me because I had to sleep with the lights on. The night before our wedding, I was asleep in a guest bedroom at his parents' house, and I had a nightmare. He got angry with me and...he was embarrassed, so the next day he left me."

"I'm not Cole," Mick said, wishing he could find the man and throttle him. "You can trust me, Lorna." Then he tried another tactic. "And because of you, *I've* learned to trust God again. I want to thank you for that."

She didn't speak for a while. Then she said, "You came back here, for me?"

"Yes, I sure did. I drove for hours and then walked through all that water, just to find you."

"God sent you." She said it again, as if to reassure herself that this was real.

Mick closed his eyes again, thanked God. "That's what you told me that first day, remember? You have to believe that, Lorna. God brought us together, to heal each other."

He heard her sobs again, this time soft and muffled. "Can I come in now, Lorna?"

He didn't wait for an answer. Instead, he opened the door and saw her there in the corner, huddled beneath clothes and blankets, her green eyes wide with fear and doubt, her long hair flowing out around her face as she held her parents' portrait tightly in her arms. The sight tore through him with a delicate clarity, like shards of tattered lace moving through a rainstorm.

Mick stayed on his knees, one hand on the door. With his other hand, he reached out to her, the light behind him guiding him. "Lorna, take my hand."

"I...I don't think I can."

"Yes, you can. I love you, Lorna. I love you, and I want to marry you. And if you want to sleep with every light in the house on, that's okay by me. But I will always be there by your side. You'll never be alone in the dark again."

"How can I be sure of that?"

Mick held his hand out, almost touching her. "You're just going to have to trust me on this. Trust me and trust God."

"He sent the rain?"

"I believe he did."

"He sent you?"

"I sure hope so. I know because of Him we found each other." He inched closer. "And I fell in love with you."

She stared at him, her gaze locking with his. "I fell in love with you, too." Then she lifted her hand toward his. "Help me," she said, a single sob shuddering down her body.

Mick closed the space between them, took the portrait away and pulled her into his arms. "Lorna, I love you so much."

"I love you, too," she whispered, tears falling down her face as she clung to him.

Mick held her there for a while, then gently lifted her body away from his. "We have to get out of here now. Are you all right?"

Lorna nodded. "I am now."

Mick helped her up, then turned to the open French doors. "Listen. The rain's stopped."

The beautiful silence fell over them like a soft chenille blanket, warm and reassuring.

"I think we're gonna make it," Mick told her.

Together, they went out onto the upstairs gallery. Then they heard a shout from below.

"Lorna, are you in there? Are you all right?"

"Lucas, is that you?"

"Yes. I'm here now, love. We found Tobias high up in a tree. He's safe and sound with his momma."

"Lucas?" Lorna called to her brother again, watching as he pushed through the foot-deep waters below. "We're up here. Mick's with me."

Lucas stopped, a shadowy silhouette there in the center of the garden. "Thank God for that."

Lorna turned to Mick. "Yes, thank God for that."

Mick pulled her close and kissed her. And again promised God that he would love her and stay by her side, always.

Through sunshine and rainstorms.

And all through the night.

Epilogue

Three months later

"It was a beautiful wedding, love."

Lorna stood with her new husband, smiling over at her brother. "Thank you, Lucas." Then she reached up to touch Lucas's cheek. "Why so sad?"

His dark eyes searched her face. "I wasn't there, *belle*. I let you down the night of the flood."

Glancing up at Mick, Lorna pulled out of his embrace to tug her handsome brother close. "Don't be silly. You saved Little Tobbie's life. Doesn't that count for something?"

Lucas nodded, then let out a sigh. "I'm thankful for that, but…we made a promise. You, me and Lacey. And I didn't live up to that promise."

"Hey, man, that was a long time ago," Mick interjected, a hand on Lorna's arm. "You can't be everywhere at once, Lucas. You did the only thing you could do. You had to find Tobias."

Lorna sent her husband a loving look. "Mick is right. For a very long time, we depended on each other so much. We forgot that God is the one in control. Lucas, we have to let go. We have to keep the faith."

Lucas nodded, then lifted a tanned hand to the white bow tie at his neck. With a grimace, he unlaced the knot. "Maybe you're right. But...something shifted inside me the night of the flood. I think I finally realized...I'm tired of remembering." He gave an eloquent shrug. "And yet, how do I forget?"

Lorna's heart went out to her brother. Ever since the flood in the early spring, Lucas had blamed himself for leaving her alone in the mansion. Now, as he stood here in his cream-colored linen suit—the one she'd insisted he wear to give her away—she could tell that he was still suffering. And not just from that flood.

He had changed. Despite his lighthearted banter, there was a melancholy surrounding him like a dark aura each time he stopped smiling.

She had to make him see that everything had happened for a reason.

Looking around, she saw Lacey talking quietly to Aunt Hilda and Justin. Although her sister looked as

serene as ever in her sky-blue bridesmaid dress, Lacey, too, seemed different since the last storm.

They all had changed.

Or maybe Lorna was the one who'd changed;
maybe she was just imagining things in her newfound
glee. Her sister had been so relieved to find Lorna
safe and sound in Mick's arms the night of the flood,
but now they'd all have to adjust to Lorna's marriage.
And Lacey had been so busy helping to prepare for
the wedding, she probably hadn't even seen that Lucas was still worried about not being able to get to
Lorna that night.

Well, Lorna wouldn't bring that up to Lacey today.
Today was her wedding day, and she only wanted
those around her to feel as wonderful as she did right
this minute.

Pulling away from her brother, the gathered skirt
of her stark white linen wedding dress rustling as she
moved, Lorna stared up at him. "Listen to me. All
this time, I thought I was afraid of the dark. I was
terrified of things I couldn't see. But it was the memories, Lucas. It was the memories of things I *had* seen,
that haunted me." She turned to Mick, reaching out
a hand to take his. "In reality, it wasn't so much the
darkness I feared." She stopped, took a deep breath,
smiled at the two men she loved. "It was the light,
Lucas. I was afraid to live in the light."

Lucas's eyes, midnight deep and just as mysterious,

held hers. "And now you've found the light with our Mr. Love?"

"Yes." Lorna laughed, then threw her arms around her brother. "Yes, I've found the light."

Mick watched as his wife hugged her brother tightly. She looked like something out of a dream in her sleeveless wedding gown, with her hair cascading from underneath her mother's perky white straw hat—the "something old" Lacey had found in the attic and cleaned up for Lorna to wear.

But she was real. This was real. Today, Lorna Dorsette had become Lorna Dorsette Love. Lorna Love. He liked the sound of that. He loved her.

"We love each other," he told Lucas. "And...I can promise you this, friend. I will never leave her alone, night or day."

Lorna nodded. "I'm all right now. I know I've still got some issues to work through, but...I'm so very happy."

"Okay, okay," Lucas said, raising a hand in defeat. "Then I'm happy for you. And I'm happy for that sap Josh, too."

They all laughed as they glanced over at the other bride and groom standing in the still-recovering summer garden of Bayou le Jardin. Josh had married his Kathryn.

The double wedding in the chapel had been Lorna's idea. And Aunt Hilda had insisted on having the reception in the garden, in spite of the continuing cleanup and replanting.

"That 'sap,' as you called him, can't be any happier than I am right now," Mick told his new brother-in-law. "And to think, he's going to train to become a real fireman, too."

"Maybe chief one day," Lucas said with a nod of approval. "The village needs a good strong, willing soul to take on the new fire department."

"I'm losing a good man," Mick confessed.

"And you're moving to a new location," Lucas countered, pointing to the big house behind them.

"No, I'm moving home," Lucas told him, his gaze scanning the gardens. "I didn't have anything holding me back in Mississippi, and I can get back there anytime if they need me."

"Right now, *I* need you," his wife told him. "I'm ready to start our honeymoon."

Lucas chuckled, then winked at Mick. "Can't turn that request down, now can you, brother?"

Hours later, as the moon glowed a creamy yellow over Bayou le Jardin, Mick stood at the foot of the four-poster bed in Lorna's room. "I'm glad we stayed here for our first night. It seems right."

She was all dolled up in something long and silky, with just a breath of the lightest shade of green in the shimmering material, to match her eyes.

Those eyes held his as she smiled up at him. "And

tomorrow, we'll be on our way to our new life. New Orleans…and then I get to show you Paris.''

"I've always had a hankering to see Paris.''

"But not tonight.''

"No, not tonight.''

"Mick, turn out the light and come to bed.''

"Are you sure? We can leave a lamp on.''

"I'm sure. I know I'm safe with you. Safe at last.''

"I'm glad you feel that way.'' He stood there, feeling a sense of awe. "And I'm glad you decided to become my wife.''

"I didn't have a choice there,'' she replied. "Remember, God sent you.'' Then she reached out to him.

Mick took her hand, then turned out the bedside lamp.

And moved toward the light of her smile shining through the shadows.

* * * * *

Dear Reader,

Have you ever been afraid and alone in the dark? As children, we often had bad dreams that sent us running to our parents for comfort. That's the way it is with the Father. He is always there to offer comfort, if only we look for the light of His love.

Lorna Dorsette had forgotten that even in her darkest moments God was still there with her, acting as her guiding light. Her fears became insurmountable, so she was afraid of the darkness. Then along came Mick Love, a simple, hardworking man who saved her not only from physical harm, but also from the dark fear deep inside her soul.

Together, Mick and Lorna had to rediscover God's guiding love and His everlasting protection. They found their own secret pavilion, and there in the moonlight they regained their trust in God and found a love that would carry them through even the darkest moments.

I hope this story brings some light to your life and I hope you'll look for the next book in the IN THE GARDEN trilogy, the story of Lucas Dorsette and the woman who finally captures his carefree but badly bruised heart. Their love brings both of them *Something Beautiful.*

Until next time, may the angels watch over you while you sleep.

Lenora Worth